RICH, NEVER MARRIED, RICH

SONDRA LUGER

Gotham Books
30 N Gould St.
Ste. 20820, Sheridan, WY 82801
https://gothambooksinc.com/
Phone: 1 (307) 464-7800

Published by Gotham Books (date published March 2022)

ISBN: 978-1-956349-06-1 (sc)
ISBN: 978-1-956349-07-8 (e)

Library of Congress Control Number: 2021925147

TO LILLIAN LUGER,

My Wonderful Mom

Suzanne Margot grimaced at the well-tanned hair shirts eying them in the lobby of Hotel Riche. She absorbed the reproving look of her absent, all-seeing, all-knowing mother, but her expression remained unchanged. The old Decca *Goyescas* was no more. What had once been "Tender Words of Love" had become "Flattering Words," a sad commentary on progress, the veracity of the translation notwithstanding. A toothy grin struck her from a few feet away.

"Sickening," she muttered, sharply turning her head away from the sight.

A mass of long, brown hair swirled to a side. Betty had looked up from the reservation form on which she had been scrawling.

"What's sickening?" she asked anxiously.

"The possibility that it's too late to find that old Decca LP."

Betty sighed her relief. "Thank goodness. I thought it was those blockheads on the sofa watching us. We need you in good spirits, counselor. You're our substitute for bourbon on the rocks."

"Why am I always used?" wailed Suzanne in mock dismay.

"Better us than them," said Nancy, steering her after the bellhop and their bags.

"Chaperoning two grown women is not my idea of a vacation."

"Yes, Zanny," chorused Betty and Nancy.

Suzanne Margot paced their luxurious suite. So perturbed was she that she failed to notice they were in the lap of imitation Queen

Anne, and when she rolled her eyes toward the usual approximation of heaven they did not record at all the trompe l'oeil ceiling. Her spirited denunciation focused solely on her plight.

She pointed her finger accusingly at Betty. "If you hadn't lost your heart and a two-week's paycheck to that horrid man with the goatee I might not be here now."

"Yes," sighed Betty. "I was doing so well, too. It's been over a year since I ran through the streets in my underwear to beg Alfonso not to break our engagement."

"There was no need to remove your clothes," said Nancy severely.

"I thought it might excite him."

"The only person it excited was Mama. Having to bail her own daughter out of prison!"

"Noble Nancy! Mama was thrilled with your indignation, you turncoat, solaced by your elaborate words of comfort, and not fooled for a minute! You wish you had the guts to do half the things I do."

"Like have five broken engagements?" taunted Nancy.

"Stop it!" Suzanne petulantly stamped her feet on the floor. "I'm the one who should be angry! I'm the one who gets stuck shepherding you two around!"

"But you're not angry, are you Zanny?" coaxed Betty.

Zanny Margot tapped her foot impatiently on the floor. "Queen Anne, indeed! What a leg!"

"Oh, Zanny, Zanny, what would we do without you!" croaked Betty close to tears.

Suzanne plunked resignedly down on the sofa. "I'm more concerned with all the wonderful things I could do without you!" She held out her arms and a red-eyed Betty and blanch-faced Nancy ran to her.

The telephone cut sharply through the stifled sobs and blubbered appreciation. Suzanne extricated herself from her sisters' embrace and reached for the receiver. She spoke not a word, but her face mirrored incredulity, annoyance, and anger in turn. She slammed the receiver into its cradle and paced again.

"Let it out, Zanny," urged Betty.

"No, I won't!" exploded Suzanne. She continued pacing.

"That's the trouble with you," said Betty.

Nancy gave her a silencing look.

And on the elder Margot paced, forward and backward and backward and forward. Suddenly she stopped and stamped both feet purposefully and repeatedly on the floor.

Betty and Nancy looked at each other and nodded. "Oh," they said.

"Lacked the decency to apologize."

"Considering your words and your tone, I'd say the lady's response was quite decent."

"But she didn't respond."

"Exactly."

"Not because she's a lady, Harry, I assure you. That breed is obsolete. And that petulant stamping—you call that ladylike?"

Harry chuckled. "She's probably a young girl locked in her room by Mama so that the likes of you won't get at her, pacing, pacing in impatient expectation of release."

"The likes of me? Really, Harry, it's more probably because the likes of me associates with the likes of you! Anyway, young girls do not take kindly to being jailed. They climb out windows or ride down mail chutes or free themselves with some other extravagance. Your decent young lady is probably a whore, stood up by her rich client and facing the prospect of paying for the facilities here herself."

Harry shook with laughter, only his tightly curled hair resisting. He removed his lanky form from the low-slung chair and stretched.

"You know I only allow you the indulgence of laughing at me because I feel sorry for you, Harry."

"Not another lecture, George, please! Save it for the conference. Phil and Derek should be arriving about now, so think about them, think about our work, and stop upsetting yourself about a female stomping on your head."

"That doesn't deserve an answer."

"Ah, blessed quiet!"

George's voice hardened, as it did when emotion threatened. "Don't you intend to dress for dinner?"

"Yes, father."

"I'm only two years your senior, but I act my forty-six years and suggest the appropriateness of your acting yours."

"I meant," said Harry Bellemore gently, "that you are the father of this conference."

"Well, somebody has to lead."

An amused smile lit Harry's face and his eyes crinkled.

"Yes," he agreed. "Perhaps the woman upstairs?"

An indignant George yanked at the doorknob, nearly missed, and half fell backward. In a fury of dignity, he pointed a short forefinger toward the hall.

"Good evening, Mr. Crump." Harry Bellemore bowed from the waist.

It did not occur to George to feign a kick at the departing backside of his friend, though in his place it would most certainly have occurred to Harry. He slammed the door shut and eyed the ceiling maliciously.

"Stupid female!" he muttered.

"You mustn't fuss so, girls. You want to notice them before they notice you."

"What do you mean, Zanny?" asked Nancy.

"I mean that surprise attacks are the most effective kind, and that you can't attack effectively until you've sized up the quarry. You know very little about these men."

"But you know, Zanny," said Nancy.

"Knowledge by proxy is not the way the wise deal with volatile substances."

"Well, we know that they're rich, reasonable-looking and presently unmarried," piped Betty.

"That's not enough," insisted Suzanne. "You can't discover everything by looking, but by their eating habits, their walk, their dress, their general demeanor, you can make some judgments."

Nancy looked thoughtful. "The eyes are very revealing. I'll look into their eyes, if I can get close enough."

"Oh, I can get close enough," said Betty merrily.

"No!" Suzanne stamped her foot.

"Better watch that stamping, Zanny."

Suzanne flushed. "You will not make fools of yourselves, of me, or of Mother."

"Oh, Mother!" Betty waved the thought away.

"Yes, Mother! You be more respectful when you speak her name!"

"Yes, agreed Nancy. "Be more respectful of the mother who provided us with all this ammunition."

She opened a portfolio packed with clippings. She cleared her throat. "George Crump, Chairman of the Board, Oil Company of America, has announced the discovery of important oil fields on company property in Tangier, where he keeps a home, etcetera, etcetera. George Crump, feted by employees on the occasion of the fiftieth anniversary of the winery established by his father in Rioja, Spain, where Mr. Crump, for reasons of etcetera, has a summer home. George Crump established first nursery in the nation for children of etcetera. George Crump—"

"George Crump, George Crump, George Crump! Get to the meaty stuff!"

"Well, let's see." She skimmed, spoke, and tossed papers aside. "Rich…never married…rich…owns three Rolls Royces, a cabin cruiser, a yacht, a jet, a helicopter, etcetera, etcetera. Rich. never married…rich…rich…rich. Short, squat, brown-eyed, rich."

"And all yours. Next."

Nancy shot a pained look at her older sister.

"*I'll* take him," said Suzanne.

"That's not the idea, Zanny. She always—"

"And *you* always, and *I* always. You both should have done your homework."

"You were always the better student, Zanny."

She sighed. "And this time, Nance, it's got to pay off. I must have a life of my own. And I won't have one until you girls are happy. Translation: married." Her voice dropped two octaves. "Maybe not even then. Mother."

"What was that?"

She laughed lightly, one would almost have said hysterically if one did not know Suzanne Margot. "Nothing, nothing. Just the ruminations of an aging maiden. You may discontinue your selective reading, Nancy since Big Sister knows all, or at least that the print made flesh does not necessarily yield the expected results. First, meet these men, talk to them, give your hearts and minds something to consider."

"Betty will use her heart and I will use my mind."

"And a cold shower."

"You don't deserve to be our sister!"

"Probably not. I should have been Princess Anne's."

"Girls!" Suzanne rolled her eyeballs toward the trompe l'oeil. "Are we wearing clothes for dinner or are we going naked?"

II

he dining room was noisy and crowded, and George Crump was not pleased. This was not an occasion for observing the social amenities. They did not need to preface their meeting with a gourmet feast, the attention of solicitous waiters or public exposure. This was a secret energy conference, not the professed college reunion and not a Cherries Jubilee. He had been a fool to listen to Harry. George Crump looked up from his napkin to watch the charge of energy that was Harry Bellemore stride toward his table. His anger at his friend was tempered, as usual, by his admiration of him. In business, he acted on insufficient evidence, followed hunches, and took risks, yet his losses had consistently been on the order of a blown feather. In his social life, even the feather remained unruffled. A wistful twitch appeared at the corner of George Crump's mouth.

"Phil's flight from Paris has been canceled—strike—and Heathrow Airport's fogged in." Harry Bellemore sat down.

"I knew there would be complications. When will they arrive?"

"You always expect complications. They'll arrive as soon as they can. Waiter! Menu, please."

"We can't start without them."

"I don't intend to diet for the next ten or fifteen hours, and I don't recommend you do, either. Drop those pounds some other time."

"You know what I mean," said George irritably. "We have rehashed our positions, our options dozens of times. There is nothing for us to discuss. If I were back at the office—"

"—you wouldn't be ordering one B & B, Fettucini Alfredo, coffee, mousse, and port."

George cast an unfriendly look at the waiter. "And I'm not. One fruit cup, two hard-boiled eggs, a pitcher of orange juice, and coffee."

Harry Bellemore put down the stick of celery he had absent-mindedly begun to nibble. "What would you do with your time, George, if you knew you had just twenty-four hours to live?"

"Know of a plot to kill me?"

"A definite, premeditated, carefully planned plot. You hatched it in infancy and you've been mercilessly pursuing it ever since."

"Let's just eat, Harry."

The food arrived and they ate.

The dining room was crowded with halter necks, glitter, bead-choked bodices, and gathered bouffant shoulders—what matter if they were last year's fashion—their suggestive contours catching the male eye, the disapproving female stare being of no consequence. Harry Bellemore whet his appetite with these provocations. At home he dined facing a copy of Modigliani's "Seated Nude." The real was unavailable, a part, undoubtedly a cherished part, of some man's private collection. The real was always closely held and unavailable, he mused. One simply had to make do with the glamour, the sophistication, and the innocent, eager, upturned face. The Bellemore eyes made a slow circuit of the room. They stopped and he laughed.

"We've been noticed, George."

"Wha-at?" George turned with alarm to follow his friend's gaze.

"Only women, George," Harry said with a touch of sarcasm. "Three tables from the second window to the left of the entrance."

"Betty, you must keep your hands in your lap."

"But I've gotten his attention, Zanny."

"Not his respect," warned Nancy.

"With all the women here looking like chandeliers, how else was I to get noticed?"

"Dear Betty has been reduced to long distance flirting and to dressing like a Danskin Lady Godiva."

"But he was looking at me." Harry Bellemore was almost upon them.

For a moment George Crump contemplated escape. Then he removed his tortoise shell eyeglasses from his inner pocket and steeled himself for what would surely be an agony of interminable chatter, simpering non sequiturs, exaggeration, and profound silence—his. Therefore he was surprised—no, shocked—when Harry returned minutes later, alone. George motioned to the waiter for coffee. He said nothing to his friend; he would kindly allow him to wash his embarrassment away in the cup. But catching Harry's mood out of the corner of his eye, he realized that he was sullen, not shamed. Across the room the female trio seemed oblivious of their existence.

"It's all right, George, it's all right. It was merely that watchdog in pink cotton, that she-wolf. The girls are delightful young things, couldn't have been more willing to join us. But that dragon…"

"An unusual animal, eh, Harry?"

"A pack of them, none civilized."

"Very pretty, Harry?" He pressed his glasses more firmly against his eyes to see.

"No one to get eyestrain for," he responded indignantly. "Those girls need help."

A faint smile played about George Crump's mouth. Pink cotton, a she-wolf, a woman. He lifted the cup to his lips and thought of the thoroughbred greyhounds waiting for him at home. The coffee tasted very good.

"She's a fool, Zanny. Let her go." Nancy Margot put a restraining hand on her sister's shoulder. She looked at the faint line that lightly marked the area to the left of Suzanne's mouth. It was clearly defined now, as it was when she became tense, as it was often lately. "Betty was born to make mistakes. She's fulfilling her promise, and there's nothing you or I or Mama can do about it. We've got to look out for ourselves and chalk Betty up to destiny."

Suzanne smiled a hard, grim smile, and the line beside her mouth deepened, but she said, "No. I can't do that. *We* can't do that. We're a *family*, Nancy!"

"What if I could prove that Betty was illegitimate, or adopted, or just a guest whose parents conveniently forgot to call for her on the way home from their vacation in the Far East?"

"Nancy!" But she smiled warmly, and even the sight of Betty accosting Harry Bellemore during his exit from the dining room and brazenly stepping between him and his friend, giving her back to the latter, even this did not erase the smile, the rising flush making it even more attractive.

George Crump looked her full in the face, a daring act for him, but daring acts at thirty feet did not faze him. He did not wait for Harry Bellemore, but with the same quick, sure steps with which he had begun his exit, he completed it. The two young women did wait, until Bellemore and Betty, still in rapt conversation, had left the room.

The lobby was filled with animation—dancing duos, trios, and quartets of color splashed across the chandelier-lit expanse.

"Look! There's George Crump leaning against that Roman column."

Suzanne nodded briskly. "We owe him an apology."

"Sorry, General; that carries responsibility too far, and my performance would never pass muster. Anyway, it would kill any chance I've got to land the Frenchman or the Englishman. George would mention my name, they'd make assumptions, and I'd be stuck with the one-syllable man. Derek, Philippe—there's music in those names, the lilt of tinkling coins—gold, the promise of charm, good looks, good looks, good—"

"I have the idea. Would you rather check The Disco Room for Betty?"

"And have her see I'm alone? Definitely not! I'll resume the reception desk stake out. That cute clerk has been most cooperative so far."

Suzanne watched her sister march off with determination, and made a mental note to remind her that inner resolve did not always make for attractive movement. She threaded her way to the Roman column, aware that George Crump, glass in hand, was watching her approach. Despite the drink his calm, untroubled gaze unnerved her.

"I—you must forgive my sister!"

He smiled. "My friend's behavior is no less reprehensible. Your apology is unnecessary," he said coolly.

She nodded her willingness to accept this. "Thank you for your understanding."

"And thank you for your thoughtfulness, for standing up to Harry, for that most becoming blush. Won't you join me for a walk on the grounds, for a drink, for—" But she had long since gone. "Crump, you are an—" But a fit of coughing over some misplaced brandy put an end to this inner monologue.

Lanterns lit the undulating garden paths, the fragrances of Givenchy and Dior emanating from bushes and shrubs in place of crocuses and daffodils asleep for the night, their senses shut to their reflected glory. Suzanne often mused thus, her philosophical bent having kept her in the past from anything but a superficial participation in the noisy parties that were de rigueur for girls "on the make." Even the relatively quiet house parties supervised by her mother and her cooperative band of daughter-laden friends had to her mind failed to realize in quality what they had failed to realize in quantity. Her easy recognition of the foibles of her fellows kept her from succumbing to the allure of their quackery. And yet, she had not retired completely from the melee. Human frailty intrigued her, and this interest in its display was, she knew, her own. She had never been in love, such a turn of mind would not allow it, and her discernment assured her that she had aroused no more than a feeling of curiosity in certain male breasts. She had convinced herself long ago that it didn't matter, but she admitted uneasily that she wasn't sure what did. Once she had done her duty, her seemingly endless duty by her sisters, she would find out. The curved arms of a bench invited her, and Suzanne accepted this offering in the semi-darkness. "This is what it means to grow old," she thought. Her mind yielded to the sound of the rustling leaves, to the sight of the light-dappled foliage and the changing shadows on the path nearby.

How long she had sat this way she did not know, but Elysium was shattered by voices, not of any order of angels or of any of nature's evening progeny. The voices were human, although Suzanne immediately withdrew from them the honor of that designation, so angry was she. Only a few feet separated her from a vulgar demonstration of wanton passion. The shameless murmurings of desire, the struggling shadows—a cheap trick—the high squeal. Suzanne stood up, mortified. Betty Margot and Harry Bellemore! Courses of action raced through her mind, none of them constructive. Bellemore would never marry Betty. She was a fool, an idiot! And the remaining trio of energy magnates would treat her like rubbish, a fate she richly deserved—and which had happened so often in the past with lesser lights that Betty was not likely to suffer remorse for long. She was incorrigible! Suzanne took a pad and pencil from her bag. Perhaps reading the kind of dialogue she ridiculed in romance novels would bring Betty to her senses. As long as these two, these two—creatures—did not exceed the decent boundaries of indecency Suzanne would not interfere. But she would write—every word!

The moon was now directly overhead and Suzanne's arms, covered by a thin shawl, were cold. Her feet, motionless for so long, felt stiff. Apparently Betty was not going to yield to Bellemore. Perhaps the chill or some wayward scrap of common sense had decided the point for her. They turned in the direction of the bench. Suzanne grasped her only exit option. The path back to the hotel would render her visible to the couple. Removal to a distant portion of the garden and a search for another route back was the only viable alternative. She turned, forcibly colliding with George Crump just as Betty and Harry Bellemore emerged from the shadows.

"Really, George!" he exclaimed in a tone of undisguised revulsion.

Betty smiled broadly.

George Crump, who had just grabbed both Suzanne's arms in a successful attempt to steady her, shared her look of incredulity and vexation.

Crump and Suzanne walked in silence back to the hotel. She cast a sidelong glance at him, and the somber face, its eyes cast unswervingly ahead, was not reassuring.

"Had you been standing there long?" she asked.

"Long enough to hear the dialogue and to see your transcription of it." He did not turn his head.

"I'm no common snoop, if that's what you're thinking, and I wasn't enjoying myself, believe me. Those preposterous words read back to her may have some effect on my foolish sister."

"What you mean to say is that Harry Bellemore's words may hold him liable to honoring the lucrative commitments he made to your sister, with your testimony as witness."

"That is most unkind!" declared Suzanne with vehemence.

"Unkind, but true, is it not?"

"Apparently you are unwilling to admit of any other alternative."

They had reached the hotel steps.

"Unless, of course, the notes were for your personal instruction."

"That is a gross and contemptible conjecture."

"Well, then." And he left her standing there.

Suzanne marched up and down the room. A soldier would have admired her precision. She could not remember when she had been so furious. Betty had dared, Crump had dared, and she had dared, and fallen so far in her own esteem that it was almost insufferable to think about it. Bellemore's promises were such that he would find it cheaper to marry Betty than to keep them. She could be a witness. Crump had heard them; he could be a witness, however reluctant. A husband at any cost! Horrible! A nightmare! Whatever had possessed her to remain there, to take notes? And what of Nancy? She, Suzanne, had destroyed Nancy's chances with any of the four men. Crump and Bellemore would see to that. What must Crump think of them? What must he think of her! He could not know of her legal training, could he? What could she do to salvage her shredded reputation, to make it all right for Nancy, to give a positive cast to the revolting activities of Betty?

She heard a key in the lock and Nancy bounded into the room in spirits the antithesis of her own.

"Zanny, he's wonderful!" She twirled around once. "So intelligent; he knows everything about the business!"

"Who?"

"Charles, the desk clerk."

"Well, why not."

"Zan—are you all right?"

"Fine," she lied.

"He's charming, personable, and very much the gentleman," continued Nancy. "Tomorrow is his day off, and he wants to spend all of it with me. Let me, Zanny, until the others come. You can trust me. Anyway, if Phil and Derek see me with someone else they'll be more interested. The biggest turnoff is the girl alone."

"It seems he's not the only one who knows everything about a business."

Nancy clapped her hands and laughed; "Darling Zanny, is it all right?"

"You won't disgrace me or Mother?"

"No-oo, not very much."

"Well—" The telephone rang. "Hello. No, this is not she. My sister is not 'available' as you put it, not now or ever, Mr. Bellemore. Good night."

The door of the suite opened and Betty sped into the room. "Was that call for me?"

Suzanne did not answer. Instead she turned upon Nancy and announced firmly, "You will not spend tomorrow with your desk clerk. You will do exactly as I say and so will *your* sister." "*My* sister!"

"You're both here in my charge, and you will not go gallivanting off on merry escapades."

"But Zanny," protested Betty, "when opportunity strikes—"

"Your kind of opportunity strikes death blows, and I'll have none of it, none of it, do you hear?" Her voice broke, but it carried the unmistakable weight of authority.

"Well what do you expect me to do," Betty responded angrily, "pull up a rocking chair next to yours, play Parcheesi?"

Suzanne stared hard at her middle sister.

"I-I'm sorry, Zanny. I didn't mean that, honest I didn't. What activities did you have in mind?"

"I'll have a list ready as soon as I take care of another matter. I'll need to be alone for that."

"You're the boss. No one enters this room until you give the word."

"And now for the first order of business," said Suzanne forcibly, as the door closed behind her sisters. And she buried her face in the pillow and cried uncontrollably.

"George, you old devil, I should be angry with you; in fact I was angry with you, but I may have been mistaken. Was I?"

George leaned heavily on the counter, facing Harry's image squarely in the barroom glass. "Not sure what you mean, Harry."

"I mean that she-devil—drawing her off me and Betty. You did consider it a sacrifice, old boy, didn't you?"

"Something in-between."

"You're selling yourself short, George; you can do much better. All you lack is confidence. I can't understand why at least a little of my example hasn't rubbed off on you."

"My example hasn't affected you."

"Amen to that. But if you're interested in joining the family fun, why not the youngest Margot? Margot the Elder would fly into a royal rage!"

"Hate her that much, do you?" George half-turned toward his friend in interest."

"More! This Stone Age viper, this ancient relic must be faced with incontrovertible proof of life in the twenty-first century. Only personal experience will teach her that."

George gulped down the last of his whisky. "Sounds like you're the man to give her the experience. You've got the passion and the noble intentions. Think I can manage both the youngest and the eldest?"

"A brilliant idea, George!"

"I was only kidding."

"A brilliant idea, nevertheless. Shall we work on it?"

George rose unsteadily to his feet. "Help me to a phone, Harry. Got to contact Phil and Derek. If they're not coming soon, I'm going home."

"I thought she was kidding when she said 'I'll take him.' Remember when she said 'I'll take him'? Of course it's not hard to believe that the stocky Mr. Crump would be interested in our svelte Zanny, despite those lines."

"They're barely visible," corrected Nancy dutifully.

"Well, that's what I meant. In spite of them she's a prize, and almost a generation younger. But for Zanny to accept him…It can't be more than sheer desperation."

"She has to be sensible. After all, she is thirty-one."

"Really, Nancy. This is not Victorian England. Zanny doesn't have to marry. I don't think Zanny really wants to marry. She's making a big mistake."

"I wonder where she learned to do that."

"Look Miss Smarty, I'm behaving as becomes a bride-to-be."

"I can't believe Bellemore has proposed."

"Why not? But he hasn't actually. He came close, though. Close enough to offer me a house in every major city in the world, and an entourage of servants to go with them, and all the clothes and jewels I desire, and oh, I can't remember the half of it."

"It sounds as if you could."

"We were about to sit on a bench and have a serious talk when we bumped into Zanny and George. I was amazed! Except for his money, Crump's no prize, but if Zanny wants him I want her to have him. I want her to be happy. But she's not happy. Do you believe the way she just spoke to us? Like a shrew! It's Harry's doing, of course. He greeted George as if he were lower than whatever it is that's the lowest. I'm afraid that Harry hates Zanny. That shooing away from our table did tremendous damage to his ego. Whenever I mention Zanny's name he gets a dark, forbidding look on his face. And Harry's approval is important. I look up to him, every woman in every room he enters looks up to him, and most important, George looks up to him."

"Hmmm, that could be it, but we ought to make sure. It won't be easy getting Zanny and Bellemore on friendly terms."

"Well, *I'm* sure. I've got a stake in their friendship too, you know. Harry is not likely to want a sister-in-law he detests. There must be some way we can get them to tolerate each other."

The bedroom door opened and Suzanne emerged. Her hair was tied at the nape of her neck in a bun, and her features were composed, serene. She wore her plainest pink robe with no collar, no ruffles, and no trim. Her hands were folded before her, and she seemed sternly at peace.

"Sit down, please," she ordered.

They did.

"What I am about to say may pain you both, but you are to listen quietly and do as I say, nonetheless. You are in my charge. Violate my instructions and you will be on the plane home before the day is over." Respectful silence. "You are here to get husbands, not to have a good time. You do not get a husband by behaving in a fashion similar to announcing the fact over a loudspeaker. Nor do you get one by making yourself freely available or making intimations thereto. You get one by being cautiously yourself, by being cautiously open to suggestions, by hesitating in the face of doubtful choices and seeking counsel. You are cautious in all aspects of this serious business until the business is consummated and in some ways, if you are wise, forever more."

"As objective observer you're tops, we don't question that. But your lack of hands-on experience does tarnish your credentials somewhat." Betty spoke softly, and she did not look at her older sister.

"I want no part of that 'we.' You don't have to be an artist to appreciate art. Zanny's advice makes sense to me."

"Romance is emotion, love is emotion. Sense has nothing to do with it. You have to understand the heart, the soul, the body."

"You have to understand Mother's reasons for sending you here," said Suzanne firmly. "They were practical reasons, but you can't deny that Mother remembers romantic love."

"Dimly."

"I have the plane schedule right here."

"All right, all right. Any other instructions?"

Suzanne unfolded a piece of paper. "We play tennis tomorrow morning at 8 o'clock on Court Four. Mr. Crump and Mr. Bellemore have booked the adjacent court. At 9 o'clock Nancy will be at the pool reading a news magazine."

"I turn intellectual."

"George Crump likes the pool but hates the sun, so he should come by at about that time. Nancy, you will act the real you. Betty, you will arrive at 10 o'clock with a backgammon set. After pretending to scout the area for a suitable player, you will settle on a voluble old lady, 90 if she's a day. I've been told that she's an avid backgammon player and her lounge is in the row opposite the men's. Mr. Bellemore will come by, be impressed with your consideration of a senior citizen, and possibly rescue you from further display of it."

"But what if my Harry doesn't come?"

"He loves the pre-noon sun—"

"Very unhealthy."

"—and will be there. We eat lunch at a large table on the terrace overlooking the pool. That will be at 1 o'clock. The hostesses will steer no one to our table but our men, should steering be necessary. There's a beauty contest on the terrace at 2 o'clock, so the men are likely to eat there. After, we leave them to a little freedom." Betty guffawed. "Them, not us. We will be exploring our luxurious surroundings for possibilities Mother may not have been aware of. We are to return to this room by six to compare notes and prepare for the evening."

"Zanny, you sit on the lounge with that magazine. I don't like George Crump."

"You'll sit and read."

"What if this little scenario of yours doesn't work as planned? Have you any infallible backup plan or do we waste the day?"

"We waste the day. Now off to bed, both of you. We breakfast at six in our suite."

"Nothing scheduled for breakfast?" chirped Betty.

"Only food, dear."

III

t arrived promptly at six. A mustached waiter wheeled it in. The doors that led off the living area were closed, except for one which was slightly ajar. The waiter dropped the passkey into the pocket of his white jacket, stood uncertainly in the center of the room and stole toward the inviting door.

Suzanne sat before her mirror. The soft, morning light lay across her shoulders, displaying the pale smoothness of her skin. Through the thin, white gown came the gentle assertion of her shoulder blades. The milky flow of movement toward the mirror and away came rhythmic and sure. A slight turn of her head revealed the classical outline of her face, the elegant features, the dazzling sheen. Her right eye, intent on outlining its partner, caught sight of a movement at the door. She half turned toward it, the filmy white on her shoulder falling abruptly away.

"Close the door please and wait; I'll be out in a moment." Her voice, low but decisive, cut through the morning stillness.

The waiter did as he was bid. He stood in the middle of the room, a towel over his arm, looking somewhat lost. He eyed the three doors, his eyes coming to rest on the one he had just closed. "The lady or the tiger?" he asked himself. "The lady and the tiger," he responded. He stood there looking at it, silent, thoughtful. And he did not smile.

Suzanne came through the door in her practical pink robe, no warm light playing on her skin, no suggestive contours visible through the loose fabric. The waiter stood more erect, clicked his heels together and bowed. He raised his head to Suzanne's dark gray eyes, to the peach porcelain of her cheeks. He felt compelled to speak.

"I did not knock too loudly, señora. I did not want to wake the family. Stupid, of course. How else could you know to open the door. Excuse me, señora. Next time I knock louder; it is proper. My wife, she is having a baby soon, very soon. My mind is not my own. My apologies to you, señora, to the señor, to the children, excuse me, good morning." He was about to bow himself out of the room.

"Just a moment, uh—"

"Pedro."

"—Pedro." And she pressed a bill into his hand. "I hope your wife makes you a father soon, perhaps before tomorrow morning?" She breathed it softly, warmly, without malice and just the slightest twinkle in her eyes.

The waiter stood in the hall. It felt drafty after the drowsy warmth and dream-like charm of the room from which he had just been expelled. Had she nudged him out the door, had he gallantly removed himself from the premises without suggestion, had he actually left the room? Yes, that he had, although he could not be sure of how. His last memory was of the irresistibly ravishing upturned face of Suzanne Margot and of his irrepressible urge to fold her to him and meld his lips with hers. Surely he hadn't done that; he felt no bruises, saw no scars. He began to walk. She had done nothing. He had done nothing. He entered the elevator. The room had wanted air and the sunlight had tricked him. She was plain. She had been plain all day yesterday and until his entry into her suite this morning. She was plain still. He entered the hallway. She had demonstrated a wicked disposition and a nasty mind. It had all been clear yesterday; it was clear still. She was an autocrat, a despot, a menace to youth, to freedom, a vixen, a termagant—. He caught himself. Well, perhaps not yet. But tomorrow she would reveal herself as such. When he delivered the breakfast tomorrow he would see etched in her face all the horrors for which she had been bespoken. He took a deep breath. He would deliver no breakfasts tomorrow; he would not meet with her privately tomorrow. He pulled the mustache from his face. He had forgotten today, forgotten his clever impersonation had been at Betty's behest, forgotten that he was to have knocked at the third door on his left and had a thrilling tete á tete cum silence with that vivacious young lady. He had forgotten everything! He quickened his steps. Suzanne had deliberately bewitched him. Betty's opinion of him would plummet; Suzanne would be crowned victor. He shook his head forcefully. It would not be; it could not be. He entered his room. A cold shower would clear his head, provide him with an explanation for Betty, a suitable comeuppance for Suzanne, and the vitality for an early game of tennis. He would call for George in half an hour; he couldn't wait until 8 o'clock. It wasn't like him to lose himself like this, and over the plainest, most stomach-churning female he had ever met. And he wasn't likely to lose himself again, he thought, as he slammed the shower door behind him.

Betty surveyed empty Court Five. "Tennis at 9 o'clock; what a splendid idea!"

"It certainly is," said Suzanne with forced good cheer. "I'll give you some warm-up serves." She appropriated the court beyond the net. Standing behind the base line, she paused to prolong the feeling. She had her own sweep of clay and the silence was broken only by an occasional rustling leaf, a stray bird, and the steady pong of tennis balls from other courts. Tennis whites dotted the landscape. She tossed the ball in the air—surely Romeo and Juliet had met on a tennis court—and swung.

"Let ball," sang the duo.

The next serve cut down the middle of the court and Nancy scrambled hopelessly for it. "It's only a game, Zanny. We want to make it to lunch."

Practice proceeded at a moderate pace thereafter. Suzanne covered the court with the ease of long-limbed experience and skill. Her graceful sprints, dodges, and leaps created a charming rhythmic pattern of their own. Beyond the fence separating this world from another, a man in loafers watched. His eyes rarely left the figure of the Amazon in white, or so his mind had dubbed her. He absent-mindedly and uselessly brushed a shock of red hair from his face as he followed her moves. Her shots were excellent, but obviously gentled for the pair across the court.

"That's it, girls!" Suzanne shouted across the net, and she ran down the foul line toward them. "Have a good game. I'm leaving my racket propped up against the fence, so a part of me will be watching you. Remember, a little exhaustion is healthy." She turned toward the fence, barely suppressing an exclamation of surprise.

The man smiled and tipped an invisible hat.

Betty's mouth fell open. "Aren't you"—Suzanne fired a sharp look at her—"a tennis star?"

"Not yet," the English voice informed them, "but a little practice with your admirable coach here and that might yet be. Might I persuade you to stay?"

Suzanne openly surveyed his person. "How do you plan to defend yourself against my serve?"

He laughed. "By serving first. But since I am racketless at the moment, would a spot of breakfast do?"

"It did admirably—in providing us with the energy for this. Perhaps we can accommodate you later, if you're still of the same mind."

"I hope the royal "we" is meant to refer specifically to the royal you."

Suzanne's eyes seemed to meet his, framed by the rough and tumble rush of ruddy hair, but from the corner of her eyes she saw the anxious, eager face of her younger sister. "Make it 4 o'clock, unless you become otherwise engaged."

"Deuced if I do become otherwise engaged! What do you take me for?"

"A man." And she hurried off before he could utter a word.

He watched the graceful swing of her hips in retreat, her long legs, her flowing hair in wonder. "A female animal of the first water. She didn't even ask my name!"

"Would you like to know hers?"

He colored. "Yes, I would." "She's Suzanne Margot, and she's our older sister," provided Betty.

"Not a headhunter, for sure, but a man eater all the same."

"Oh, men are not her thing. There's a mutual apathy between them," continued Betty. "She's dedicated to her work and her family."

"Is that so. I'm Derek Barnesforth. And you ladies?"

"Are Betty," the speaker pointed to herself, "and Nancy Margot."

"How nice that you vacation together. Close family ties have rather gone out of style. Pity."

"Do you often vacation at American resorts, Mr. Barnesforth?"

"No, Betty, only when I am informed that three charming sisters will patronize a given hotel, and that is a rare occurrence. Some friends of mine were to play on the adjacent court. Perhaps you saw them?"

"No," hurled in Nancy. "We hoped the court would be occupied, but no one came."

The scathing look Betty gave her was caught by Derek.

"Then you know Harry and George?"

"Only slightly," offered Betty.

"Ah, well, then a better acquaintance is certainly in order. Where can you ladies be found today?"

"At the pool in an hour, at the patio at 1 o'clock for lunch," said Betty with assurance. "There's a beauty contest on the patio at 2 o'clock."

"The three of you will certainly make it difficult for the other contestants."

"Oh, we're not entering."

"But Nancy, you should, you should. I doubt if three more attractive women are to be found on the premises. Doubtless I'll see you at lunch, but please remind your reluctant sister of our engagement at 4 o'clock."

Where the tennis path intersected the pool path Derek Barnesforth was faced with a distant view of his friends disrobing in the morning sun. The umbrella had given them away. George was the only man he knew who took the sun under the shelter of an umbrella. Harry was lavishly slapping the contents of a bottle of suntan oil on his body as he approached.

George jumped to his feet and grasped both of Derek's hands in his. "Derek, thank goodness. Now we can begin."

Harry Bellemore threw a casual hello at the newcomer. "We can't start without Phil," he said lazily. "You said so yourself."

"Yes, we can. We can fill him in on our progress later. We can't afford to waste more time!"

"Why not?" countered Derek.

"I'm not wasting all this oil or this sun." Harry lay on his back and adjusted the shades over his eyes. "Pull up a chaise, Derek, my boy, and soothe us with an account of your intrepid journey here. Are you there, George?"

"Yes," said George disconsolately, "I'm here."

"You're holding *Newsweek* upside down," whispered a voice behind the cover of the magazine.

"Oh!" Nancy sat upright in fright, blushing profusely.

"Oh, I know, I—" She looked at the magazine. "It is *not* upside down."

"For all the reading you were doing, it might just as well have been." Harry Bellemore appropriated the foot of her chaise. "Actually, the news reads better that way."

"Would you care to read a section?" she said coolly.

"Not really. I just came over to get a better look at those gorgeous legs."

Nancy blushed red again.

"Here," he said, pointing to the advertisement on the back cover of the magazine.

Nancy tore the back cover from the magazine and thrust it at him. "You're welcome to them," she said with more than a touch of pique.

Harry Bellemore stared long and hard at the legs in the ad and the legs on the chaise. "A striking resemblance," he decided.

But Nancy was not to be mollified. "Betty won't be here for another half hour, so you might just as well go away."

"I'm not looking for Betty."

"Mr. Bellemore, I don't mean to be impolite, but I'd like to read this article."

Bellemore stretched his length along the unoccupied side strip of the chaise. His arm over Nancy's head dangled by her shoulder.

"What are you doing!" She scrambled off the chaise.

"I thought we could read together. I wasn't about to attack you. I simply wanted to be friendly. Or is that too much to expect of family."

"Family!"

"Actually, I spoke more in hope than in truth."

"Are you saying that Betty won't have you?"

"For a casual liaison, yes, she is more than willing. But I want more serious a commitment than that. I've had enough amusement in my life. Now I want a—a—a—"

"A wife!" Nancy concluded in awe. "But Betty would marry you in a minute."

"Pretense, all pretense. How can I believe she means it? I've seen those looks, heard those sighs, those words so many times before. It's all pretense."

Nancy stiffened. "I'm thinking that you may be the one who is all pretense, Mr. Bellemore. Excuse me."

And so it happened that when Betty arrived with her attache of backgammon Nancy wasn't there and Harry Bellemore wasn't there. However, the expectations for 10 o'clock had not gone completely awry. The old lady was there. Betty sat down on her lounge dejected. Just because Zanny kept her own dull life in order didn't mean she could impose order on an exciting life, or one that would be exciting if left to function on its own, thought Betty. What did Zanny know of passion or love? All she could offer her sisters was a combination of sympathy and severity, which Mama apparently felt sufficient propellants to success for her two marriageable daughters. For a moment Betty felt the insane urge to run away from the script, from Mama, from Zanny, even from her shadow Nancy. To let her boss find another slave to type his letters; she had been rebuffed by him often enough. What a resume of experience she had—five jobs in three years; she could get another job in a snap. Another job, her own apartment, another coterie of men! But she couldn't do it. Mama's tears were ready at the merest threat of such events, as were recounting of her romantic experiences as a young woman bereft of mother, and therefore of reliable female counsel. Sometimes Betty purposely implied rebellion to hear again the stories that filled her with such awe and admiration of her mother. She never used her widowhood to elicit compliance, making Betty feel all the more keenly the injustice of disobeying this special woman who lacked what she, Betty, longed with singlemindedness to achieve. So she was trapped, trapped by affection and obligation to do as Big Sister, Mama's stand-in, said. Even from twenty feet away she could see the old lady shake as she turned the pages of her magazine. Someday she would break away, she vowed. She glanced hopelessly around her. A scattering of people lay on lounges under the cloudless sky. The two-tiered swimming pool contributed the sound of whooshing water falling to the level below. The old lady shaded faded blue eyes to view the person at the foot of her lounge.

"Do you play backgammon?" asked the young woman dully.

"Yes, I do. Sit down." The owner of the cracked voice motioned toward the adjacent lounge. "That's why I'm out here. Until noon I play backgammon. Those nice, young men at Reception have been so kind, so obliging. They've given my lounge number to so many sweet, young people like you, dear, and to quite a few lovely, older people, too. One reads so much in the newspapers about nasty, horrid people that one would think no other kind exists, but I've always found people to be very kind. Very kind and helpful. Shall we say five a man?"

Betty only half-listened to the cracked drone of the old lady's voice. "What?"

"Five a man, dear?"

"Oh, I don't play for money," she said absently, her eyes searching first one then another route to the pool area in vain hope of salvation.

"Well, neither do I; the game itself is pleasure enough. But in honor of tradition I always make a small wager on the outcome of the game, per man on the losing court. I am an old lady and tradition means a lot to me. Would you like to guess how old?"

Betty, her hands in her lap, her eyes now looking past the old lady, said she would not.

"Perhaps a little wager?"

The old lady's glance shifted easily from Betty's face to the game as her hands, shaking but deft, completed the arrangement of men on the board. Betty had not heard. She raised her voice and the old crackle cut through Betty's thoughts.

"Five a man then, dear?"

"All right," said Betty, despairing of Harry Bellemore.

The old lady smiled with pleasure. "For tradition," she said, and said little more.

Betty exclaimed at the blots she created, at the blots that were hit, at losses in her inner table, but her ancient opponent merely smiled indulgently. Her eyes never left the game. It was all over in short order. The old lady looked up as she bore her last man off the board. Betty had been backgammoned, and easily, but the winner did not say so.

"You were not paying attention, dear. The men on the board require your attention. Another game, perhaps? Just a little concentration and you will recover your loss."

Betty stood up, stiff from the position she had assumed. "No, I don't think—"

"Just a little concentration and you will bear all your men off the board."

"No, really, I—"

"Bear all your men off the board," the voice crackled strongly. "You can win."

Betty's eyes met the faded blue. She hesitated. She dreamed.

"Perhaps a greater incentive? Shall we say ten a man? Is that agreeable?"

IV

When Suzanne left her sisters at the tennis court she went back to their suite. She showered and washed her tennis clothes, hanging them from the rod in the tub. Then she used a key on the only locked piece of luggage, removed a heavy portfolio, and settling herself into the most comfortable chair in the living room set herself to reexamining and reassessing one Mr. Derek Barnesforth. It was not an unpleasant task. Mr. Barnesforth was not an Englishman of prim and proper stripe, as was the atypical American Mr. Crump. Nor was he the exaggeration of the irresponsible American playboy, as was Mr. Bellemore. He was more the all-American boy from the other side of the ocean grown to middle age, a blend of tousled good looks and youthful daring. She looked at the photos her mother had clipped. There was Mr. Barnesforth hosting a travel writers conference, judging an exhibit of the ten most promising young artists in Devonshire, leading the pack in the Barnesforth Charity Steeplechase, "a family tradition since 1912." And there were the women. At debutante socials, yacht christenings, charity balls he was shown with a different beauty on his arm or at his side. One was dark and exotic, another blonde and demure, and still another red-haired and vivacious. It was almost as if the little boy at the counter had taken one of each variety of the most prettily-wrapped candies without partiality for any, taken them and passed them on. Suzanne turned to the biographical sheet that her mother had compiled on the man. His father had given him as step-mother a famous actress, his mother had given him as stepfather a financier, and his sister Jennifer, a nun, had given him her blessings. Derek Barnesforth had attended Oxford and Harvard, with majors in music, art, and business administration. He had become in rapid succession vice-president in charge of research, vice-president in charge of exports and, two years ago at the age of thirty-eight upon his father's assumption of the position of chairman of the board, president of British Oil Company. He was a creative and responsible man and if he could be gotten he would do splendidly for Nancy. They were complements and contrasts and would make a suitable match. Mr. Barnesforth would find this out in due course. Nancy merely had to be told.

Margots did not argue about the necessity of marriage and could not afford to argue about the choice of mate. They were either pretty, like Betty and Nancy, and in competition with multitudes of other like-featured American girls, or plain, like Suzanne, and in competition with the world. "If he is wealthy and likeable, he is a suitable match. After marriage, at your leisure, you may fall in love." So spoke Mama. And Mama knew. Mama had been in love often in her youth. None of her loves had been wealthy, but, as she had pointed out, they had had the prospects. They had been ambitious, determined young men and this, in addition to other charms, had catapulted Mama into love with them. Or at least what she had understood love to be—an irrational delusion that caused her to neglect her duties at home, put on clothing inside out, forget her resolves of an instant before, and laugh heartily at her father's timeworn jokes and even at the perfunctory "good morning." The lawyer-to-be had been superseded by the doctor-to-be who had been superseded by the business-tycoon-to-be. All had been superseded by Papa. Papa had said that he owned property in twenty-five states and in Spain, that he had parlayed one thousand dollars in stock market investments into fifty times that amount. Papa had lied. Mama blamed her gullibility on inexperience and lack of the invaluable counsel of a mother; she had been only nineteen. The prospects of her earlier suitors had been genuine. She had had no reason to believe that Papa, her father's admonitions notwithstanding, with his easy manners and money and his self-confidence, would be a fraud. After their marriage she used his devotion to her and his pliability to win for them an approximation of the wealth she had anticipated marriage would bring. The best she had been able to do was achieve a state of comfort for their growing family. Papa had been willing to do better, but his aggressiveness proved to be only drama-class deep. And so Mama had languished in comfort, determined that her daughters would reap the reward of her dreams, her expectations, and her experience. Why had Mama not married one of the young men with prospects? Impatience, she averred. She had assumed that Papa was already rich. With men she never assumed again. Mama had done her homework. Scrapbooks of carefully culled clippings and copies of printed material on the world's wealthy bachelors, in mint condition, divorced, widowed, testified to this. Mama read a wide variety of publications regularly, from business magazines to gossip magazines, for she never knew when or where information about prospective sons-in-law might appear. Mama was thorough and, as a consequence, extremely well-read. Suzanne had spoken with her mother about computer technology and labor, the stability of the Swiss franc, the future of Hollywood studios, and the financial success of fashion houses in New York, Paris, and Rome. Primary learning for attorney Suzanne and collateral learning for Mama, who was even knowledgeable about the sex drives of the Zulus, information garnered in pursuit of the facts about a wealthy young anthropologist. And Mama was fully aware, grimly aware, of the sexual mores of the time in general and of the men in her scrapbooks in particular. But sex was beside the point to her. It was induced by a state of mind, like love, but money was concrete and the marriage contract tangible. Love was the whipped cream on the cake, sex the sugar icing, both nothing without the cake they adorned. Yes, she knew that marriage was not "necessary" these days, but for her daughters it was necessary. Yes, she understood that at a time when more and more people had less and less to put on their tables cake was of secondary importance, but it was of primary importance to her girls. Young people were turning increasingly from pursuit of wealth to pursuit of an irresponsible "happiness," but her girls would not turn from it. Her daughters would marry well and eat cake. She willed it to be so, and she was working doggedly toward that end.

Suzanne replaced the portfolio in the luggage. If all had gone according to plan, Betty was at this moment playing backgammon with Harry Bellemore and Nancy, bored with the magazine and George Crump and upset at seeing Betty with Bellemore, had stolen away to find excitement of her own, hopefully not with the desk clerk, not until the afternoon at least. Mother would not approve of even that much liberality. Suzanne would make sure that Nancy had not appropriated the morning for her hotel-tycoon-to-be. She gazed out the window of their carefully chosen room. In the distant left lay the pool, cabanas, and outdoor dining areas. She searched for the pinpricks of color that would identify the members of her clan. She identified Betty playing backgammon with the old lady. None of the male trio was in sight. Nancy had already gone elsewhere. The entrance to the tennis courts revealed none of the people who interested her. Staring at the lush greenery she visualized a possible course of action for the remainder of her morning and pictured fleetingly the possible results of the plan her sisters were to follow until evening. Organization was the order of the day, every vacation day, until it yielded the desired results. The security of organization. What a comfort! Suzanne frowned, and the hard line appeared at the corner of her mouth. The pictures faded into the luxuriant shrubbery, into the magnolia trees and the opening stretch of path that honeycombed the hotel. Into the shrubbery indeed! Her eyes flashed. "For though there are some disagreeable things in Venice there is nothing so disagreeable as the visitors." She nodded her agreement with Henry James as she tossed a volume of the author's travel essays into her handbag and headed for the lobby.

V

The young desk clerk was not there. The only people in the lobby were those in transit. A balding man signing in at the desk stared at her. He was not Philippe Juneau. She looked away. She decided on a corner nook which provided a view of all entering and departing and of the all-important desk. Juneau's flight had landed half an hour ago at the local airport. He would be checking in soon. Something about the Juneau clippings had been unsettling. It was more than his three marriages, his centerfold playmates, or his quick temper. It was something left unsaid in accounts of him, something vaguely disturbing. She didn't know exactly what it was, but she felt the urgency of witnessing his entry and making a judgment before her sisters did. Bellemore with his equally reprehensible play life she detested. But something about Juneau went deeper, Something darker, unstated but implicit in those clippings, gave her concern. She thumbed through James' Venice, London, Paris, Warwick. So many adventures to choose from, so many imaginative escapes from the here and now.

"Hi, I've been trying to place you."

Suzanne looked up into the face of a boy barely past his teens. "We've never met," she stated flatly, and returned to Henry James.

"I'm sure we have," he persisted. "What's your name?"

"Anon."

He thought for a moment. "Were you at the rock convention in Miami in March?"

"No, I wasn't." She lowered her eyes to the book.

"Henry James!" he said, forcing animation into his voice. "You have a taste for philosophy, then."

She could not resist a response. "You're thinking of William James."

From the corner of her eye she saw his shoes. She sat up with a start. Philippe Juneau had entered the lobby.

"Yes, of course, the one with those erotic ideas."

"You mean Henry Miller," she said, half-listening. She watched Juneau advance to the desk.

"Do I?" He twisted a shirt button below an expanse of hairy chest. "I—I suppose I do."

"Please move to a side, you're blocking my view."

He moved to the left.

"No, no, the other way," she said with irritation.

He moved to the right.

Juneau had given her his back. She studied his stance, his posture, his precision movements. He did not bend to sign the register; he raised it to the wall to make his entry.

"Then who is Henry James?" He flung out his arms, blocking for an instant her view of the figure at the desk.

Suzanne could not contain her exasperation. "Will you go away!"

"Sure, just trying to do a good deed. You're not hot stuff, you know." And he hurried off.

The bellhop was leading Juneau away. Suzanne rose abruptly; the urge to follow them was keen. Where was his luggage? The bellhop carried nothing; Juneau had entered the lobby with none. She quickened her pace. Had it preceded him, would it follow him? Why? Her forebodings increased. Juneau was aristocracy in motion, tall, erect, sharply economical in movement. But he was not aristocracy. He had been born of peasant stock, orphaned, and adopted into the good life, into society, into wealth. He was an anomaly, not all that unusual in the nouveau riche, but still…The duo slowed. Suzanne pressed her back into the wall of a corridor niche and cautiously peeked around the bend. The bellhop was handing Juneau the keys and pocketing his tip. Juneau unlocked the door, and for a second his shoulders seemed to lose their starch. Then he disappeared inside. How she longed for Charles, the desk clerk! He could perform yeoman service with a master key. But of course he had more frivolous concerns to pursue, off in the stacks with Nancy no doubt. She looked at her watch. In forty-five minutes she would meet the girls for lunch. If only the men did likewise! If only Juneau's room were available for inspection at that time! She would have to find Charles. He wanted time with Nancy and she wanted information and a key. She grimly determined on some minor concessions.

She traversed the extensive grounds twice before she saw him sitting under the shade of a giant tree, his arms clasping Nancy, his face one with hers. Suzanne waited impatiently. The passing seconds were surely minutes. How could they breathe! She searched for a rock, found it, and was about to hurl it through the nearby trees to attract their attention when a steel grip wrenched her wrist in mid air. She turned around to face Harry Bellemore.

"You don't want to do that," he said quietly. "You might hurt someone."

"Like you, you mean! Let go of my arm!"

Bellemore removed the rock from her hand and released his grip on her wrist.

"You are no gentleman!" She massaged her wrist.

"And you are no lady."

"I'm more lady than any you've ever known."

Bellemore seemed amused. "Does that include Betty?"

Suzanne responded with such a resounding slap that the embracing couple broke apart and jumped to their feet.

Bellemore's eyes blazed. He gripped both her wrists in his. "Is the gentleman going to get violent?" flung Suzanne. Bellemore cast her hands away from him. "You are the most unnatural, unprincipled, irrational excuse for a female it has ever been my misfortune to meet."

"I am unprincipled?" Her voice ascended, shrill.

"Are we interrupting something," offered Nancy.

"Not at all. My wife was merely polishing her public image on my poor person." He anticipated the slap and ducked. Charles caught it on the side of his chin. Suzanne was horrified. "Oh, Charles, forgive me!"

"Forgive?" questioned Bellemore, stepping back as Suzanne lay indignant eyes upon him. Nancy was all concern too, and the effect was not disagreeable to Charles.

"You'd better sit down," urged Suzanne.

"Isn't that what started all this?" asked Harry Bellemore.

"Will you please leave us?" Suzanne was controlling her voice with visible effort.

"Since the request was worded so politely, and since Charles seems to be enjoying himself, I will honor the request. May I suggest, however, that at this moment Charles would benefit more from ice than from another romp in the grass?" And having had the last word, he was gone before Suzanne could wound him with a response.

"That impossible, pugnacious, revolting man!" Suzanne shuddered.

"What were you doing with him here, anyhow?"

"I wasn't doing anything with him, Nancy!"

"That accounts for his rage," said Charles.

Suzanne clenched her fists and said nothing. She paced up and down among the trees. Charles and Nancy watched quietly, waiting for her to stop.

Charles could wait no longer. "He was trying to upset you. You needn't cooperate with him so completely."

Suzanne stopped pacing. "That's part of the reason I'm angry."

"Are Nancy and I the other part?"

"Should you be?"

"I don't hurt ladies; I respect Nancy."

"What page from what book," wondered Suzanne, but she had no venom left to dispute his assertion. She would speak to Nancy later. "Let me see that chin. I'm truly sorry, Charles."

"Oh, that's all right. Any time I can keep customers from tearing each other apart I will. Hotel Management I." He grinned.

Suzanne's brow crinkled. She thought, "I can't ask him to violate hotel rules now. How childish of me to have lost my temper, and toward whom? Ugh!" That last found its way to her lips.

"Oh, it's not that bad Zanny. He could use some ice, though."

"I guess Mr. Bellemore was right, then," said Charles.

Suzanne bit her lip. Why concern herself with Philippe Juneau? Until her fears were allayed Juneau would be off limits to the girls, that's all. They had enough to contend with. Betty had more than enough. They made their way back to the hotel. Mr. Bellemore was right, then. She swallowed hard. Mr. Bellemore might have to be right often if Betty were to make this very suitable match. "I'm mature enough to control myself," Suzanne scolded silently.

As Harry Bellemore hurried to the pool in search of Betty his thoughts echoed Suzanne's. He would not get on with Betty if he antagonized her older sister. She held the purse strings and full authority over the Margot brood, and Betty had made it clear that while she was willing to bend the rules she was no longer willing to run the risk of outright rebellion, which could result in her prompt departure for home. Amicable relations were out of the question, but kindness was not impossible. Yes, kindness would be the best revenge. It would bring surrender. Beautiful! No woman was going to thwart the achievements of Harry Bellemore. He met Betty between the cabanas and the pool. She was visibly upset.

"Betty! Forgive my note. I would have rushed to you myself, but after the message you sent me I was sure you wouldn't listen. A man of honor should not forget a rendezvous with a scintillating, unforgettable vision. I thought of you all night; sleep was impossible. I couldn't wipe you from my mind and the clock—"

"Oh, Harry, you're so wonderful! I think you're the only one who really thinks of me at all! All I get are instructions, orders from an antiquated point of view, and all they lead to are trouble! No one cares about my needs; everyone is so selfish!"

Bellemore nodded solemnly, his tussle with Viper Margot still fresh in his mind. "But I care about you; even when my memory plays the villain I decidedly, unalterably care about you." This did not quell Betty's distress. "Is anything else the matter? Can I do anything for you?" His voice was tender, solicitous.

Unmindful of the crowds, Betty threw her arms around Bellemore. "Oh, you're wonderful, wonderful!" She released her hold. "But I can't ask you to. I'll be sent home in a snap, even though it's Zanny's fault. *She* told me to play backgammon with that fossil, but I'll get the blame." She wiped her eyes welling with the makings of a deluge.

Bellemore made comforting noises, put his arm around her shoulders, and lowered her into a chair. "Now, now, it will be all right; just tell me what happened."

Her voice held back the tears. "What happened was that I got ripped off by a decrepit old lady. 'Let's play for five a man, for ten a man,'" she mimicked between sobs. "Well Zanny said play, so I played! I thought she meant ten cents, but she meant ten dollars. I owe two hun—Oh, Zanny will kill me, Mama will kill me. I'll have to pay them back, but my credit cards have been canceled and—"

"Shush, shush. Let me understand you: You lost $200 gambling with an old lady."

"It was $225! She wants the money in cash hand-delivered to the lounge."

"Where can I find her?"

"She's still at the pool. What she's doing must be illegal; I mean rip-offs can't be legal, can they? But who would believe me except you, darling Harry, except you. She hasn't even got a name. She's listed on the lounge chart as 'old l-a-d-y.' The employees must get a percentage! Oh, Harry!" Her arms enveloped him once more and the tears fell.

Bellemore could not avoid a triumphant smile, which he turned into a scowl as he gently pulled her from him. "I could pay the loss"—she drew him near—"but I wouldn't want you thinking I was paying for any favors." She pulled back. "Anyway, I don't hold you as cheaply as that. If the loss were a thousand times that amount then I would begin to consider paying it. But I'm very good at talking sense into little old ladies. I'll see what I can do."

"Oh, Harry!"

He offered her his handkerchief. "Where can I find you later?"

"Lunch on the patio at 1 o'clock and the beauty contest after."

"The prospect of seeing you in the contest will give me added courage to tackle the old lady."

"Oh, but I'm not entering."

"There goes that extra margin of courage."

"Zanny wouldn't hear of it; she's against undue exposure."

"A concomitant of her wanderings at the North Pole."

"She's gotten me out of scrapes before. I couldn't embarrass her, I just couldn't…"

"Well, if you couldn't…Let me attend to our aged harpy."

She watched him go, dubious of his success. You couldn't talk to old ladies. Now if he had offered the $ 225 itself…He was such an idealist!

VI

She lay in the shade of the umbrella, her eyes closed, "Is that you, Harry?"

"You're sharp as ever, Leticia. How are you?"

She opened one eye, "How do I look?"

"You look just fine. George didn't mention you were coming."

"George didn't know," she crackled. "I suppose I'll have to tell him now, won't I." She opened the other eye.

"Have you been too naughty for the hotels at Palm Beach?"

"It's so tiresome to be called naughty, Harry. I've never known a child as clever as I. Why must clever people over the age of forty be forever called naughty. You're the cleverest of the lot of George's friends. Shall I call you naughty?"

"I shall never call you naughty again."

"Thank you, Harry. You always did respond to common sense. Where's George? I hope he took his vitamins with him this trip. Young people are so forgetful, you excepted of course."

"Then you know I won't forget to ask you whether you're still on the wagon, as you promised me, as you promised George, as you promised the desk sergeant at Palm Beach."

"I haven't touched a deck of cards for a full year, except to play solitaire, which I've played solitarily in my own home."

"Poor, dear Leticia, has it been a strain?"

"Of course it's been a strain, you silly. Try dispensing with those cigarettes you cling to as if they were Sophia Loren."

"I would hope to have the sense to cling to Ms. Loren some-what differently."

"You know what I'm talking about. In no time you'll be my age and have trouble merely raising those blasted pieces of stuffed paper to your lips, let alone rising to the challenge of Ms. Loren."

"Aren't George's lectures enough?"

"No, mine are better. George would never think of Sophia Loren as a cigarette. And my wisdom, the product of many years of living, mind you, gives me the right to advise you."

"You've never advised George to marry, quite the contrary."

"You know George isn't ready. It's not a matter of years. You've been ready for ages, but you foolishly insist on enjoying yourself. The day will come when you won't and then no one will have you."

"With my money? I doubt that Leticia. I can be sans teeth, sans hair, sans hearing, and some young lovely will still want me for my money. Nothing will have changed."

"Well, don't be too sure. I'm sans quite a few things myself, but I see no flood of men lining up before my lounge."

"Only young ladies who play backgammon?"

"So that's it. I should have known you would pay me no mind otherwise. Do you wonder that I take whatever pleasure I can when-ever I can?"

"Leticia," he wagged his finger at her, "you know that next to young ladies, George, my company, my employees, and our labor union, your company pleasures me the most of anyone in the world."

"You dog!" She grinned a mouth of teeth minus three.

"And who taught you to play backgammon? Not for a moment did I suspect that you were plotting to use it against me."

"But Harry dear, would you rather I toyed with the meager savings of the elderly? That would be too cruel of me. I can't believe you would have me do that. Of course, dear, I would avoid your friends, but all young things seem to be in that category. I'm entitled to a little enjoyment, a little reward for surviving the vicissitudes of life this long."

"When George finds out—"

"Oh, you wouldn't report me to my own son!"

"Would you rather the authorities did it again?"

Her face fell, and the hollows in her cheeks showed clearly. "Who's the girl?"

"Betty Margot. May I tell her you are canceling the debt?"

"Not even five minutes to savor my victory." She sighed.

He bent over and kissed her on the cheek. "Thank you, darling. I'll make it up to you."

"Really? What will you teach me next?"

"How to enjoy life without gambling."

"Well, it's been a while, but I'm willing to try again. But he must be tall and under thirty."

Harry Bellemore kissed her once more with gusto. "Remember what you promised." He signaled to a waiter. "Champagne punch for my sweetheart, here."

"I'll remember," murmured the old lady, as Bellemore strode confidently away. "I'll remember that I made no promise whatever!"

Harry opened the door to a room shrouded in semi-darkness and George's square behind bent over a briefcase. George turned his head.

"I'm glad you're early, Harry; we can set up our position papers before Phil and Derek arrive. I've ordered lunch for 12:30. Are poached salmon and fried eggs all right with you?"

"Fine, George. Did you remember to bring your vitamins?"

George whirled around. "Mother's here!"

"Yes, she's here, tanning under an umbrella at the pool, a la Junior."

"She worries about wrinkles. What is she doing here? I put her on a plane to Cannes."

"She was worried about your vitamins."

"Nonsense; she knows that I take them without fail."

"Maybe she forgot."

"Mother, forget? There are things I wish she would! Is she all right?"

"Fine."

"No—trouble?"

"Your mother is a woman of her word."

"Of many words, often contradictory. I ought to run over to the pool to see her, but Derek and Phil will be here soon."

"And you mustn't be late for your own conference."

"You're always thrusting the onus of leadership upon me."

"You're the only one who wants it. Sublimation of your erotic desires, channeling them into business creativity and leadership."

"A man can do both, you know."

"I know. Haven't I been urging you to for years?"

"I'm not cut out for bed-hopping. I need stability, a contract—business, If you like—marriage."

"Then go about it in a businesslike way. Make a list of what you need from a woman, how much, your physical specifications or pre-dilections thereto and voilá—your blueprint is ready! Have it made into a shoe and search for your Cinderella."

"Very, very funny, Harry, but I've got a simple blueprint; I'll admit it."

"In writing?"

"Yes."

"And you carry it with you all the time?"

George ignored the question. "Lay out your papers; I want to start promptly."

"May I see it? I know you're not afraid of the contrary views of a proven friend."

"Oh, well, here." George removed a slip of paper from his breast pocket and handed it to Harry.

Harry took the paper to the window. "If we don't get some light in here, our secret conference will be a secret to us, too; we won't be able to read our damned notes." He adjusted one slat of the blind so the light fell onto the paper and read: "'petite, long brown hair, blue eyes, quiet, somewhat intelligent, 35. Is that her weight or her age, George?"

George snatched the paper from Harry's hands. "Can't you take anything seriously?"

"Ah, George, when one begins to take matrimony seriously, one is in for a disappointment."

"Are you disappointed, Harry?"

"What do you mean?"

"You take matrimony so seriously you take great pains to avoid it. I take it so seriously, I take great pains to insure my happiness when I enter into it."

"So we're alike after all," said Harry good-naturedly. "But this woman you want isn't hard to find. Feed this data into a computer and you will come up with the names of thousands of women."

"Probably, but I want someone unique. This is only the outline."

"It's the filling that's the problem, then. You've got a yen for sweets and won't admit it, George. You've missed a lot, but you're still young, still vigorous, and alas, still a coward. Take my advice, George, and rip up this slip of paper. Rip it up and stay single."

"With all the success I'm having you may have your wish. But I'm not the dating type; I've never been much good at small talk, or any other kind for that matter, except business."

"Then find yourself a quiet, somewhat intelligent businesswoman."

"They don't want to talk business on dates, either."

"George, you have my sympathy," said Harry drolly. "At least alter your qualifications from time to time so you won't get bored searching."

"I do. Every year I up the age requirement by one. Originally, I hoped to marry a woman of 25."

Harry considered a laugh, thought better of it, and shook his head. "Well, my boy, I wish you happiness, as I always have, and if marriage will make you happy, then—" He was unable to get himself to complete the statement. He walked to the bar across the room and poured himself a scotch and soda. He sipped it slowly as he watched George finish the arrangement of his papers on the desk. "Were you considering Suzanne Margot?"

George looked up, amused. "You think her 'quiet' and 'somewhat intelligent'?"

"Well, she's quiet, withdrawn, reclusive, sexless when she's not defending the imaginary honor of her sisters and she certainly isn't *very* intelligent."

George smiled broadly now. "Think you've beaten her, then?"

"Betty adores me, and The Viper will soon regret her condemnation of Harry Bellemore."

"She'll come crawling to you gushing apologies, I take it."

"I don't want her apologies, and I don't want her!"

"Of course not. She's sexless when she's not protecting her sisters from you, but she seems constantly to be doing that, doesn't she?"

"She's the one they need protection against, but why waste breath on the subject?"

"Amazing how the mention of her, *your* mention of her sparks such strong feelings."

"Of disgust! There's not enough room for my papers on the desk. May I open one of your bridge tables?"

"Yes, that's what they're there for."

Harry assumed the grave demeanor of his business self and gave inordinate attention to the routine of removing papers from his briefcase and laying them out on the table. Derek and Philippe entered the room and Harry looked relieved.

"Wonderful. I'm anxious to begin this conference."

George looked at Harry suspiciously.

"There's a beauty contest this afternoon. If we get the preliminaries over with, we can adjourn to the pool at 2 o'clock to watch it, and think over our positions, of course."

"Of course, Harry! What do you say, Phil?"

"I say it's an inspired idea. Dare we ask George?"

"It's all right with me; why not?"

"Then that's settled. Drink—Phil, Derek? Orange juice, George?"

"I think we ought to get started, if we want to make the show."

"Right, George."

There was a scraping of chairs and new collections of paper appeared.

"Any fourth Mrs. Juneau on the horizon?"

"No, unfortunately, Derek."

"Three times and several lost millions later and you mean to tell me that you haven't learned your lesson yet?"

Phil parted thin lips for his response. "I like being married, Harry. Family tradition."

Harry counted on his fingers: "Uncle Max, divorced twice; Aunt Clarissa, four times; Cousin Albert, twice; Cousin Eunice, three times; Great Aunt Hattie, six times, the last at age 72, and I forget the others."

"You speak of the Juneaus; I speak of the LeClairs."

"Quite right, dating back to William the Conqueror."

Harry had forgotten what was so easily forgettable—that Philippe Juneau had been born Philippe LeClair, the only son of Louis and Agnes LeClair, who had tilled the soil in Provence much as their ancestors had since the eleventh century. Philippe was the sion of old, industrious, peasant stock and he had never forgotten, or more accurately never gotten over, the fact. Harry had tread on sensitive ground, and he regretted it. His own origins also had been humble, but in the land of Horatio Alger such a success was cause for adulation. Harry had made himself. Philippe had been made and, though his performance in business deserved kudos, he felt it keenly.

"And you, Derek, any cast-offs that might interest me?"

"What makes you think I've any to spare, Harry?"

"That hot, eh? Have you developed a system of rotation or something to account for this selfishness in the face of a request from an old friend?"

"An old friend, you say? Harry, I haven't seen you socially since our Harvard reunion eight years ago."

"And I saw Phil at Clarissa's third wedding four years ago. We've rather grown away from one another. Now, shall we begin our meeting?" George sat down with a sense of finality.

"Would you rather we were back at school?"

"Phil, that would be perfect. What a time we had then!" Derek slapped his leg.

Phil looked somber.

"After breaking our heads over the work, that is."

Philippe Juneau allowed himself a small smile, lost in the hearty laughter of the other three men.

"So, here we are, out-of-touch, middle-aged bachelors all, and if we don't get some work done, George won't let us attend the beauty contest, right George?"

George chuckled agreement with his red-haired friend as a knock sounded on the door.

"Ah, lunch, good." Derek rubbed his hands. "I hope you remembered I hate salmon, George."

VII

From the luncheon patio the pool looked like a post card picture of a waterfall surrounded by lush foliage and mosaic paths. In this setting sat Betty attempting to lecture her older sister.

"You've misjudged Harry, Zanny, really you have. You've swallowed the stories in those silly clippings of Mama's, but you said yourself that so-called facts may be contradicted by interaction with the real, live person. Interaction reveals the truth. A man can't hide what he is when you interact with him."

"And then it's too late. But I will allow that Mr. Bellemore may not be quite what he seems to be, either in print or in person."

"Zanny! That's a really generous statement for you to make. I don't mean by generous, that you're giving him more than he deserves, just that you're being open-minded and wonderful. Oh, I love you!" She gave her sister a big hug.

Suzanne accepted it passively. Betty always loved her when she believed she was having her way. And why was she giving Bellemore the multiple benefit of her multiple doubts? Why was she ignoring her instincts, her judgment? Was she recognizing the hopelessness of battling Betty's inclinations and Mother's wishes? She had her own life to consider, her own future to work for, but only if Betty were well-matched in the present. Well-matched, or the horror, the embarrassment would begin all over again, time and again, until life was no more. She was trapped by loyalty, much as Betty was trapped by emotions and her mother by disappointed dreams.

"Hi!" Charles' voice cut into her reverie. "May I join you?"

Betty dutifully looked at Suzanne.

"Of course, Charles. How is the hotel business coming along?"

"Very well. We have 85% of the rooms filled, a 5% increase over last week's figure. We've hired three new waiters and busboys this week alone."

"Won't the chambermaids and kitchen staff feel the added pressure?"

"Yes, but management has drawn the line there. You only spend money where the expenditure shows."

"You should be hearing from the union soon."

"We expect to!" Charles surveyed the five empty places at the table. "Are we waiting for Nancy and four men?"

Suzanne laughed heartily. "It's that obvious, is it?"

"Only to the eyes of management, in this case future management."

"How long have you been working here?"

"Two months: two weeks paid vacation plus six weeks unpaid vacation from my city job. If they knew, they'd probably consider me AWOL. Vacation hotels and city hotels aren't the same, though. Here you're trapped, away from activity if the hotel doesn't provide it. Country hotel management is a more intense and isolated experience. It's an experience I wanted to get."

"How old are you, Charles?"

"I'm 27."

"Mother would have loved you thirty-two years ago!"

It was a pleasantly warm day, but a touch of palpable humidity and a scattered array of fluffy clouds forewarned of a summer shower. Betty listened spasmodically to their conversation, hoping for more than a recital of business achievements and dreams, but she was not rewarded with more titillating comments. She eyed the clouds with both misgiving and hope. If Harry had done away with her debt she would be obligated to return his favor, a pleasurable obligation. One might even tear the word obligation and toss it to the wind; their intended breakfast liaison had been proof of that. But Zanny would object—strongly—and if the rain washed out the contest it would be preferable to making a decision concerning it. Betty reflected that she had been lucky. The morning affair, however adapted to her nature, had been an aberration of her performance as sister and daughter, as uneven in acceptability as she knew that to be. In short, it had been a mistake. Her mother and sisters cared about her, and in lucid and contemplative moments such as now she realized she could not count on such unswerving concern from an acquaintance of two days, even if he had promised her the world. When her natural inclinations and activities led her into the quagmire, it was family that pulled her out. She was pleased that she could reciprocate by not burdening them with another problem, and she felt some satisfaction in knowing that Zanny's information about the old lady had been dangerously incomplete and that she, Betty, had spared her the knowledge of this. Her gaze moved from the clouds to Charles and Zanny, engaged in conversation still. Naturally Charles was waiting for Nancy. It was big of Zanny to entertain him so, she decided, even as she vaguely wondered why. And where were Nancy and Harry—and George, and Derek, and Philippe?

"Where are they? It's 1 o'clock," she blurted out.

"I'm willing to search for Nancy," said Charles, "but I leave the gentlemen for your discovery." He rose. "May I return with my prize?"

Suzanne hesitated. It wasn't more than a split second, but enough for Betty and Charles to realize his tenuous status in her favor.

"Yes, if you like."

"Thank you!" he said in the tone of a man who had just been given unqualified approval.

"Where are the men, Zanny?"

"At a luncheon conference in Mr. Crump's room. But I can't say that I'm sorry. I'm ashamed to face Mr. Crump, would lose my appetite in company with Mr. Bellemore, and would rather we approached Messrs. Barnesforth and Juneau without the hearing of the other two."

"But you do like George Crump and you don't hate Harry Bellemore?"

"I respect Mr. Crump and, for your sake, I won't hate Mr. Bellemore."

"Oh, Zanny, thank you!"

Suzanne transferred her smile to the clouds. "It's so lovely here now, so peaceful, so green. And if it rains it will be even lovelier, even more restful and clean."

Peaceful? Betty viewed the bustle surrounding them: waiters jostling one another, the banging of plates, the scraping of chairs, the shouts of children at the pool. But she had long ceased to wonder at Suzanne's odd remarks. If they did not pertain to men and marriage, Suzanne was welcome to her enigma.

Nancy arrived apologizing. "Sorry, I was detained."

Betty was incredulous. "That's all? No further explanation?"

"No. I wasn't with Charles, and that's more than you're entitled to know. May I see the menu, please?"

"Well, I like that! Are you going to accept that, Zanny?"

"No arguments before eating, from either of you. They interfere with digestion."

"Poor Charles," remarked Nancy.

"Quite literally," responded Suzanne. "In ten years, with his drive and potential, Mother would agree to the match."

"But in ten years I'll be 30!"

"A horrible prospect," Suzanne agreed wryly, "so Barnesforth it is."

Nancy slipped a paper to Betty under the table.

"Excuse me," said Betty leaving the table with as much grace as haste would allow. The note was from Harry Bellemore. It read, "Talked sense to the old lady. Debt canceled."

The day had darkened. Dusk descended on the pool patio at 1:45 P.M. The cabana boys, undaunted, were completing the arrangement of extra chairs for spectators of the beauty contest. Suzanne, seated with Nancy in the back row, looked anxiously for Betty.

"She knows where we're sitting, so relax; she'll find us."

"If she wants to, you mean. Can you see Mr. Bellemore?"

Nancy blanched. Had she abetted un-Margotlike behavior? She strained to see Harry Bellemore. "I'll go look for him," she said, just a shade of guilt in her voice. She scoured the area thoroughly and finally caught sight of him and his companions in the most obvious place—the first row. Betty was not with them. Dutifully, she reported this to Suzanne.

"Something is the matter. Sit here, Nancy. I'll be back as soon as I find out what it is."

Suzanne's first stop was the telephone. Betty was not in their suite. A quick traversal of the grounds for a dead body, a new liaison, a heaven-knew-what, and a visit to the lobby to inquire for messages, all yielded nothing. It occurred to her that Betty might have left some indication of her whereabouts in their suite. In their absence the chambermaid had tidied up, but neither Betty nor a missive from her were to be found. Suzanne looked at her watch. It was 2 o'clock. Surely Betty would not have chosen to miss the beauty contest, frivolous excuse though it was for exposure. Certainly beauty was a nebulous thing to judge and the least important of attributes, thought Suzanne. It was only because she knew the men they sought would consider such a contest a major spectacle and be present at it that she had decided it would be wise to be in the vicinity of this mockery of value, not close enough to see their vulgar responses to it, but close enough to encounter them on its conclusion, when reality and a sense of the attractions of her sisters might be appreciated. On impulse she opened Betty's closet. She scanned the clothes slowly at first, then quickly. The daring décolleté gown that Suzanne had fought against bringing was gone and, horror of horrors, the nylon nightgown, imitation of one seen in a passionate, dramatic film, had likewise disappeared. Suzanne slammed the closet door shut and stared wildly into the empty room.

"Oh, my God! She's entered the contest!"

There was no time to be lost. She rushed like a woman possessed to the scene of the impending crime. Nancy sat with Charles. Suzanne barely had breath to command.

"Has she appeared yet?"

"What—Who—?"

"Come with me!" She wrenched Nancy from her seat and all but flew with her to the dressing room door. It was barred by a large, broad woman.

"You can't go in there, I'm afraid. It's too late to enter."

"Our sister's in there!"

"How nice!"

Suzanne's rejoinder was the force with which she hurled herself past the guard, dragging a breathless Nancy behind her. Inside were dozens of girls in various states of dishabille. The sisters looked about them frantically. The announcer could be heard quite clearly, despite the boom and reverberation: "Debra Darwin will now appear in a gossamer gown, copy of an original design for the film production of—" The rest was cut off by a shriek—Betty's. In panties and bra she screamed incomprehensively at the exiting Ms. Darwin, following it up with a dash after her. Suzanne and Nancy were at her heels as she entered the public arena in mad pursuit.

"My gown! She's wearing my gown!"

Suzanne and Nancy attempted to pull her back as she lunged for the filmy material encasing the clearly visible physique of the well-endowed Ms. Darwin.

The culprit swung fiercely at Betty. "Get her off me!"

Harry Bellemore jumped onto the platform, pulled the girls apart and carried Betty, still screaming, to the dressing room.

"Where are her clothes?" he demanded, holding fast to his hysterical charge.

"My gown! She's got my gown!" Betty's litany continued, her exertions for freedom gaining unnatural strength as she saw Debra Darwin enter the room wearing the purloined garment.

"Get that gown!" Bellemore thundered imperiously to Nancy, "and let's get out of here!" He made an immediate exit, leaving behind shrieking girls and general pandemonium.

A rumble of thunder had dispersed the fringes of the audience, and a bolt of lightening that followed sent the remainder scurrying for cover. George Crump darted to a canopied section to retrieve his mother.

"It's about time you came 'round to say hello," she grouched between claps of thunder. "If I'm not in some sexy situation you forget I exist," she added unfairly, as her son led her back to the hotel.

A drizzle had started, but by the time the Bellemore party reached the lobby it was pouring in sheets. Bellemore roughly brushed his way past milling guests and made for the staircase. He stopped on the first landing and put Betty, now quiet and dripping wet, on her feet.

"If this were a film, I'd carry you up, but—" He shook his head and panted heavily. "But I'll escort you to your suite." His hand firmly gripped Suzanne's shoulders as he placed her behind Betty. "For the sake of modesty," he explained, bringing up the rear. And with that futile but gentlemanly gesture they proceeded to Margot quarters. Bellemore looked away as Suzanne, key in hand, stepped in front of her sister. Betty pushed past her and into her room.

Suzanne faced Bellemore. Her wavy shoulder-length hair now lay in a glistening stream down her back, the flowery sundress she wore a severe contrast to the wan and haggard expression on her face.

"Thank you, Mr. Bellemore. I don't know what else to say. Your behavior has been exemplary under shamefully sensational circumstances."

"You mustn't think of it so," he began gently.

"Mustn't? But I must! I'm a part of this despicable, disgraceful, disgusting display! Had I kept closer watch on her this would not have happened."

"But it wasn't her fault her gown was stolen."

"She was wrong to even think of wearing such a—a thing! That was a nightgown, Mr. Bellemore, an intimate item of apparel to be worn in private. She might just as well have walked onto that stage naked—and, my God, she practically did! I'll never forgive myself!"

"You can't lead someone else's life, no matter how honorable your intentions. Betty should be allowed the right to learn from her experiences."

"Learn from her experiences, yes, and *such* experiences. Will that day ever come? She's a woman, not a child, and the sooner she recognizes it, the happier I will be."

"And what about Betty's happiness?"

Nancy approached carrying Betty's clothes. "Betty is too stupid to be happy," she asserted, brushing a lock of wet hair from her mouth.

"Nancy! Your sister is not stupid! See if she'll talk to you."

"What good will that do? She's already made an ass of herself. Some photographer has probably gotten a camera-full worthy of a dozen *Playboy* centerfolds."

"Oh, Nancy, don't even think such a thing!"

"That would be impossible," Bellemore said quickly. *Playboy* centerfolds are full nudes."

"Yes," said Suzanne icily.

"I'll check to make sure no pictures were taken for whatever purpose. If any were, I'll make sure they are destroyed. Better yet, I'll deliver them personally into your hands. I don't want you thinking I would want such photos for myself."

Suzanne blushed. "That would be kind of you, but you have no obligation—"

"I do feel an obligation," he said, remembering his request to Betty.

"Thank you, Mr. Bellemore. I appreciate that. Your behavior has been—"

"—most exemplary!" he concluded.

Suzanne laughed, and for a moment the tension was gone from her face and Bellemore saw the charm of a mermaid with streaming hair slapping her fins against the water. He did not trust himself to smile. Instead, he clasped her hands in his as farewell and left without another word.

Suzanne leaned her back against the closed door. "He feels an obligation to Betty," she murmured. "He must care about her. He didn't enjoy the spectacle any more than I did. He made an excuse for her, tried to save her from humiliation. He cares about her." She recalled his commanding presence, the way he had gripped her shoulders on the stairs. "Betty has ruined her chances with any worthwhile man here except Bellemore, but Bellemore is the one who matters." She couldn't understand why she didn't feel happier about this. There had been inadvertent method in Betty's madness after all. The vagaries of life had arranged it so. Her mind allowed Nancy's voice entrance. She heard her entreat and cajole Betty to no avail.

"She won't open her door, but she's all right, only crying. She hasn't hanged herself or strangled herself with the bedclothes. I peeked through the keyhole."

Suzanne kissed her sister. "Thank you, Nancy. Let her cry. Things have worked out well after all."

"Well? Are you kidding!"

"This—episode—has forced Mr. Bellemore's hand, or rather, his heart. He cares about Betty; he practically said so. Isn't that wonderful?"

"Are you telling me he's in love with her?" Nancy asked in astonishment.

Suzanne felt a heaviness in her heart. "Very possibly. If Betty is careful and can nurture his feeling for her, who knows."

"Marriage!" she said reverently. "Then he was serious at the lounge. He said he wanted a permanent relationship, but that Betty wanted less. I thought he was playing games. And we always thought that Betty communicated her feelings so well! Well, that little misunderstanding can be cleared up fast enough. Betty married. Won't Mama be relieved!"

Suzanne could not understand her depression. She was on the road to freedom. Betty's conquest was wonderful news.

Harry Bellemore went to his room and started pacing. He recalled how he and George had categorized the pacer above George's room: a whore abandoned and upset or a young lady chafing at restrictions and marching for release, for freedom. But he had not been abandoned; he had been embraced, and he was not yearning for release but for imprisonment, contrary to all the advice he had given George and anyone else who would listen. He laughed bitterly at the irony. He had gotten his revenge on Suzanne, a revenge with honor, and she had gotten her revenge on him. Just the other day he had wanted her abject surrender to his desire for Betty and he had gotten it. Just the other day he had sought to have her groveling, apologetic, and he had gotten it. But that she-wolf with the creamy shoulders and peach complexion would not let him enjoy his victory;

that viper with the brown mane glistening down her back would not allow it. She had bewitched him and accomplished the inconceivable. He didn't want Betty or any other woman, and he didn't want his freedom. George would be mildly disappointed, but George was not in love, so it was of no importance. The only thing of importance was to win Suzanne Margot for himself. He did not expect it to be too difficult a task to accomplish.

Bellemore left his room and took the elevator to the lobby. It had become a magnet for the guests whose pleasures had been rained out. He saw Phil and Derek at the bar and joined them. They slapped him on the back at once.

"Hail to the hero! The drinks are on us, Harry." Derek signaled to the bartender.

"Harry, she's some woman! Rectitude with guts! I haven't witnessed anything like it since I watched the climb of Mt. Everest."

"Where is George?" he asked, trying for a change of topic.

"In the corner there, with Leticia. He brought her over for greetings, but it was evident she still disapproves of us; she dragged him off almost immediately."

"She feels you were a bad influence on George, you and Derek."

"Me especially. But she has forever liked you, Harry. I never could discover how you managed it."

"Charm, and my undisguised admiration for a fighter."

Derek laughed. "As long as she's not under forty and fighting you! But talking about fighters, I hear you know that spunky little number in the bra."

"We've met."

"More than 'met,' I believe. If you're finished, would you mind if I had the pleasure?"

"Yes, I would."

"Leave him alone. You've got the older sister for tennis, Derek. It's not like you to juggle your women like that."

"A tennis date does not make Suzanne Margot one of his women."

"Rather testy, aren't we, Harry? Is the youngest off limits too, or may I venture to make her acquaintance?"

"Of course, Phil. Sorry, Derek. In my old age I'm getting to be a hog. I'll introduce you all at dinner. That's a promise."

Derek glanced at his watch. "The tennis courts aren't likely to be dry by 4 o'clock, but a gentleman cancels, however obvious the situation. Excuse me."

Bellemore watched him go with misgivings. He had the habit of reversing a minus to a plus.

"Have another drink, Harry; you're weakening. I never thought a woman could drive you to that. Which one is it?"

"Playing analyst, Phil?"

"I've been with mine so long, I rather believe I could, but your signs are so obvious that a novice could read them."

"So you think it's just one. That would indicate decline! No offense, Phil; I know how you and George feel about 'one'—at a time, at least. Come on, let's rescue him from Leticia."

Phil put his empty glass on the bar. "I'm gentleman enough not to want to step into your territory, Harry. Help me out, then. If I should find the youngest inadequate, which one of the other two am I to avoid?"

"No interest in Debra Darwin?" answered Harry evasively.

"Not even as an interlude between marriages. I've seen all there is to see of that young lady."

VIII

Nancy was being shooed out the door by Suzanne.

"Derek's invitation must not be refused. Don't you want to meet him?"

"You know I do, but it's you he's asked to meet. If you refuse now you'll only make him more interested. That won't help me at all."

"When will you learn to have more confidence in yourself?" She pushed her back into the room and to a floor-length mirror. "Look at yourself. Look at those lips, moderately full—lovely; look at those cheeks, softly molded—lovely; look at that nose, neither snub nor long, beautifully proportioned—lovely; look at those eyes, powder blue—lovely; look at that forehead—need I go on?"

"No, you've made me confident enough for the next fifteen minutes. Will that be enough?"

"Enough. Derek Barnesforth will look at my Nancy, talk to her, find out what a treasure she is, and forget my name!"

"That headache story won't wash. I'll plead tears for you brought on by Betty's exhibition."

"Strangers never think of me as the crying type."

"Neither does family, but emotion is a more convincing excuse than reason."

"If I weren't so busy worrying about what's to become of you and Betty and Mother I might have some time for tears. If you want to shed a few, by all means do, Very romantic, tears. And your freckle-faced artist and musician will love you for them. Now go!"

Suzanne gave her a final shove and she was on her way. She waited patiently for the elevator, rehearsing in her mind incidents and opinions that might appeal to a man with a yen for things romantic.

The door opened and standing there in tall, thin, regal splendor was Philippe Juneau.

"Good evening. Going down?"

Nancy hesitated.

"You know my friend Harry Bellemore."

"Somewhat," she responded guardedly.

Juneau put the door on "hold." "He has a high regard for you and your sisters. You're, uh—"

"Going up."

Juneau laughed. "I won't harm you. Harry promised to introduce you at dinner tonight, so if you would rather wait…I hope your sister is all right. Young ladies find flaunted theft hard to understand. I would imagine this to be as true here as it is in Europe. We shelter our young so."

Had Bellemore said nothing? "Betty's not all that young."

"Young enough, like you, to be chaperoned by an older sister, although you are certainly Betty's senior in discretion. It's safe to ride with me."

"I'm sure it is, Mr. Juneau," Nancy responded with minimal assurance.

"Ah, Harry told you my name, but he didn't tell me yours."

The elevator door shut.

"Nancy Margot"

"I'll see you at dinner, but I would be pleased to have you join me for coffee now."

The elevator was of the stomach-sinking kind, and her thoughts raced to match its haste.

"I can't have coffee with you."

"Well, then, I'm willing to offer you gin and tonic, but no more than that. Your sister would rightfully disapprove of anything stronger. But I would enjoy talking to you, if you would care to, that is."

"I would like to very much, Mr. Juneau, but I have a message to deliver."

"There are telephones."

"That wouldn't do, but I guess it can wait ten minutes."

"Ten minutes will be fine. The cocktail lounge should be quiet enough at this hour to allow us to squeeze twenty minutes of conversation into that meager ten."

She was young, impressionable, proper, and pretty, not the kind one took to one's room right away, which was just as well, he thought.

One must grasp opportunity when the door opens on it, thought Nancy. Zanny would agree. She might even forward her older sister's merits to George through Philippe. She would not be spending her ten minutes selfishly.

"One gin and tonic, that's all I had, honest Zanny."

"You expect us to believe that you spent over an hour with a man and had only one drink? You can do better than that," snorted Betty.

"You would be too jealous to believe the truth," Nancy shot back.

"Girls, please. There are enough men for both of you."

"There are never enough men for darling Betty. If she were a man, she'd be as footloose and free with women as her precious Harry Bellemore. They deserve each other."

"Talk of jealousy!"

"One gin and tonic, that's all I had. In the company of a man as fascinating as Philippe Juneau, who has a thought for liquor or a fraud like Harry Bellemore? He began by holding out the chair for me—"

"And you were so thunderstruck you fell through it to the floor."

"Betty, I've listened to you when you've chosen to tell me about your experiences, and you will please allow me to listen to your sister do the same."

"He wanted to know all about me, my favorite food, drink, music, hobbies—"

"Hamburger, ginger ale, rock, and man-hunting."

"That is the last interruption I will permit."

"Oh, all right. Speak on, Nancy."

"I said it all, yes I did. Well, all except the man-hunting, which you know, Zanny, is more a passion of Mama's than a hobby of mine. I admit that at first I said beef bourguignon was my favorite food, but he corrected my pronunciation and said he loves hamburger too! He was wonderful. He asked me about my job and gave me tips about getting out of the secretarial pool. He said I'm too intelligent to be merely one in a crowd."

"La-di-da. Congratulations on your success with the Frenchman. Were you able to get any information about him, or were you so enchanted with your own voice that you forgot that your intention is to marry another human being, not to fall in love with yourself."

"I found out that he's interested in me as a person. Can you say that of your Harry Bellemore?"

"Well, his heroic effort today clearly showed that he wasn't interested in exposing me to public view, which shows a bit more interest than a man who lets a gullible girl talk on and on."

"I'll wager his interest is in exposing you to his private view."

"How much will you bet? Oh, God!" The color flew from her face and her knees began to buckle.

Suzanne pulled her close and murmured consoling thoughts. "It's all right, it's all right; Bellemore cares. We all care about you, don't we Nancy."

"Oh, yes! Oh Betty, I'm so sorry. You weren't exposing much more than you would have in a bikini. You'll be married before either of us!"

Betty rallied. "I don't know what came over me. Of course everything will be fine. How can things help but be fine when my two sisters are working so hard to see that they are?" She forced a smile. "Is Philippe as handsome as his pictures?"

"More handsome. He's got these thought lines on his forehead and these character lines around his mouth, and some faint lines that crisscross his face like a subtle, elusive melody. He's all man, all gentleman, and gorgeous!"

Betty said nothing. Suzanne, finding no support in Nancy's recital for her undefined fears about Juneau, felt the imperativeness of meeting him and judging for herself.

"Mr. Bellemore phoned us an invitation to dinner tonight. Since he was kind enough to ease our minds about the beauty contest photographs, I accepted for all of us. You'll introduce us to Mr. Juneau then, Nance."

"I won't have to; Harry Bellemore told Philippe he would do that. Apparently Philippe expressed his interest in meeting me before fate brought us together in the elevator!"

"Not necessarily," said Betty, barely audibly. "Well, I suppose we'd better dress now for this evening."

"I'm going to wear yellow, with a yellow-ribboned ponytail. That should give me the young, sweet look I want." She kissed Zanny exuberantly and swept into her bedroom.

"Young, sweet look," repeated Betty disdainfully. "She's only 20. She ought to stop reading those silly romantic novels and learn what life is really about. 'A subtle, elusive melody.' Absurd! You'll have to have a talk with her, Zanny." She kissed her sister perfunctorily on the cheek and started for her bedroom.

All of 22, Betty would be the one to talk about reality. "Well," thought Suzanne, "she takes her own advice about romantic novels. She's so busy bringing their characters to life she has neither the time nor the desire to read them!" She closed her eyes and conjured the warmth of her mother's presence. Then, her mind filled with her apricot-colored dress, tortoise shell earrings, and magazine clippings, she entered her room.

"Bellemore."

"Yes, Mr. Bellemore. Your table for seven. Have your party follow me, please." The maitre d' led them to a table near the garden. The chandelier overhead cast its sparkle in the glassware.

Suzanne reflected that the elegant lighting did not suit her simple dress. Her sisters harbored no such thoughts. None of their necklines dipped to immodest depths, Suzanne had seen to that, but Nancy was enveloped in Philippe's glamour and Betty shone with Bellemore's smile.

"This is a damn fool thing to do," Bellemore told himself, as he seated himself across from Suzanne.

"No, no, Harry; you've got it wrong," said George Crump. "You sit across from Betty. What's the matter with you? You'll have to get up, Harry. You can take your water glass with you."

Harry had no choice. This presumption was beyond any he had ever witnessed in his friend. "Such an informal, friendly dinner, I didn't think it mattered," he offered lamely. The chandelier glittered above them. He observed the couples facing each other. "Ladies and gentlemen, greet your opposites: Philippe Juneau, Nancy Margot; yours Harry Bellemore, Betty Margot; George Crump, Suzanne Margot; and Derek Barnesforth—poor Derek, you are left without a tablemate for this evening because Madame Margot did not have the foresight to provide us with a fourth daughter."

"Why can't we rotate after each course?"

"An excellent idea, Derek! We men will move to our left after the appetizer."

"This is a meal, we can't play musical chairs!" complained George.

"It's unfair, Harry; the appetizer is a short course."

"We'll eat it slowly, Phil."

"Fruit cup," remarked George unnecessarily to Suzanne. "Fresh fruit is very healthy. I have orchards at all my homes. We grow oranges, grapes, kumquats, figs, dates, all indigenous varieties. The oranges at Rioja taste different from the oranges at Tangier. We don't grow any oranges in New York. Naturally." He cleared his throat.

Derek leaned across the table. "Grow any aphrodisiacs?"

"Not as such." He refused to look at Derek. "Do you have a favorite fruit?"

"I daren't answer that," said Suzanne with a grin. "Which ones are aphrodisiacs?"

"Well—"

"Derek, can't you wait your turn?"

"I don't know why you're impatient, George; at the rate you're eating I won't have one."

George dug into his fruit cup. "Grapefruit isn't ripe," he noted.

"Do you plant the trees yourself?"

"No, I haven't the time. I've resigned that task to a competent staff."

"Then at one time you did the work yourself?"

"Actually, no." George dug more deeply into the fruit. He was coming off badly.

"Delegation of power is a necessity in a successful business. Is it possible we're eating some of your fruit?"

"We don't export. The fruit is only for the family." The silence deepened. Voices from around the table and around the room were beginning to intrude on his concentration. Their fruit cups were almost empty. "I admire your stewardship of your sisters." He regretted the statement as it slipped from his mouth.

"Thank you, but as you have undoubtedly noted, I'm not infallible."

"I appreciate that, but the effort is commendable. I'm an only child myself. I've never had to assume responsibility in a personal way for someone younger. Of course, when I marry I'll remedy that."

"May you find it less nerve-wracking than the care of two younger sisters!"

"I intend to choose carefully."

Suzanne put her hands under her chin and asked with interest, "What kind of woman would you choose?"

George groped in his memory for the requirements. It would be unthinkable to pull out the piece of paper itself. "I can't quite remember. I—you—" he stumbled, "you've driven them clear out of my head!" He blushed into his dish and prayed that Harry would announce the next course. From the depth of his embarrassment he heard her voice.

"I'm honored that such a decent and respected man should think so, but I suspect the fruit has turned." Suzanne's rejoinder belied a pleasurable sensation. Despite her spying on Bellemore and Betty, despite her participation in the farce at the pool, despite her distant demeanor, George Crump liked her. She was surprised and gratified.

"Soup." The formerly fruit-laden cups were whisked away and replaced by soup de jour. The men rose and reseated themselves.

"I assumed you would esteem yourself more highly." Derek Barnesforth stared daringly into Suzanne's eyes.

"I don't believe in false modesty."

"You don't believe in accepting a sincere compliment, either. Your gratuitous and cockeyed opinion was not in good taste."

Suzanne reddened. "I will not debate the matter with you."

"Does that mean you agree with me or that you consider a response beneath your dignity?"

"It means I will not debate the matter with you." She gave her attention to her soup.

"I shouldn't wonder at that. When a woman ignores her appointments, she shouldn't be expected to adhere to any other propriety."

"I'm sorry if you feel the explanation Nancy forwarded to you was inadequate. I agree that one should keep appointments."

"Nancy gave me no explanation; what made you think she would? I sat in the coffee shop one hour waiting for you."

"Oh, Mr. Barnesforth, I am so sorry. I sent Nancy down for a personal delivery of my regrets, but another matter interjected itself and apparently she forgot her errand. I don't blame you for being angry. I'm truly sorry."

"You're forgiven. As long as *you* didn't forget. Weren't you feeling well?"

"After the events of the afternoon, I wasn't quite up to it."

"I understand. Would you be up to a game tonight?"

"Tonight? Can't it wait until morning? Perhaps we can play doubles."

"I'm afraid this is a working vacation for me, and I question whether my schedule will permit tomorrow. And I prefer singles. I find one-to-one relationships more satisfying, especially since I expect you to give me some pointers on the game. I was very impressed with your performance this morning."

"I can't refuse your request for a game tonight, then, can I?"

"You can, but hardly with grace, charm, and good taste." He touched her hand lightly.

"Entree."

At last Suzanne faced Philippe Juneau. "Another charming Margot," he said.

Her mind flitted over her performance at dinner thus far. "Don't be too sure." She capped the statement with a half smile.

"You may be surrogate mother of this feminine trio, but surely now, all softness and loveliness under a sparkling chandelier, you are yourself."

It was chivalrous nonsense, but mindful of Derek's chastisement she responded in decorous, if slightly sarcastic fashion. "You overwhelm me, Mr. Juneau." She sliced her meat and attempted to close her ears as the inevitable echo of those words came back to her. What was there in those clippings about him that had disturbed her? Not the usual false exterior, surely; she was used to men and women wearing masks. Hers fit quite snugly itself. He sat inflexibly straight and appeared unnaturally stiff. Was that what had bothered her in recent photos of him? His thinning, sandy hair was a fitting accompaniment to his quiet features and those gentle lines. Was it the posture, then, something more?

"You have the most astonishingly good posture, Mr. Juneau."

"The result of a skiing accident. Poor posture gives me pain."

"Yet you ski in spite of it, I would guess."

"I do. I love skiing. The feeling of exhilaration as you sweep down the mountain is unmatched by any other sport. I've tried them all."

"Auto racing?"

"Too far removed from nature, too industrial."

"Water skiing?"

"I prefer the brisk air and bundling up."

"Whatever do you do during the summer?"

"Heighten my admiration of winter."

Suzanne laughed appreciatively. "Your disability has affected neither your courage nor your humor."

Annoyance creased his face. "A little pain is no disability. It makes one more sensitive to people and the pain many feel so keenly in this world."

"A Provencal heritage is rich with hardship and grandeur."

"I value the achievements of both my families. The LeClairs and Grandfather Juneau made individual achievements, the one with land plowed almost since time began and the other with one gas station."

"From what I've read you have contributed greatly to that achievement."

"You enjoy following the progress of oil men?"

"Incidentally. It's more prudence than joy. I prefer to anticipate the cost of heating our home each winter."

"I can sympathize with that. I am tempted to convert my homes to solar heat, but the publicity would do irreparable damage to Juneau Oil. Like you, I prefer to be prudent."

The early pictures of a devil-may-care Philippe Juneau went through her mind. He was older now and by his own judgment prudent, despite a recent extravagant divorce settlement. Prudent—the word did not satisfy. She carefully observed the man opposite her. If looks could reveal qualities, what word would encompass both? He was regal, stately—no, those would not do.

There was a slight commotion. Betty had found something disagreeable about the entree. She rose to leave the table. Harry Bellemore's concern was immediate.

Suzanne rose, too. "No, no Betty. It's quite all right. I can live without dessert. Excuse us."

Nancy sat for seconds more. She reveled in having three men to herself. How delightfully jealous Philippe would be if she divided her attention among the four of them, as etiquette demanded she do. But she was not adroit at such things. Philippe might take offense. Worse, she might be thought callously indifferent to her sister's malady. She rose.

"I may be able to help. You have all been very pleasant, but you must excuse me."

The men, who had likewise risen to their feet, sat down. George looked at Harry's worried countenance. "It's chocolate mousse, Harry, a double portion," he said, donating his own plate, but there was no perceptible change in Harry's expression. "Betty will be all right. A little indigestion, that's all. It's easily remedied." He lowered his voice, but added cheerfully, "And you have saved yourself a course, a double portion no less, of The Viper."

Upon entering the lobby Betty made a rapid recovery.

"Oh Betty, shame!"

"You faker! I should have guessed. But why?"

"One chocolate mousse, Nancy, and my seams will burst."

"But mine won't!"

"Did I tell you to follow me? Go back to the dining room."

"I'll look like a fool."

"Then don't go back." She clapped her hands in delight. "You heard how worried Harry was that I might not be able to stay up late tonight. Why, I practically had to force him to agree to meet me outside the ballroom in an hour. Where do you find such a gem?"

"Not in your arms," retorted Nancy.

"Let's get back to the suite for a bit. It won't do to have Harry Bellemore hear that you paraded your indigestion in the lobby."

"Yes, let's get back to the room," agreed Nancy with relish. "You can supply the antidote for the child's indigestion after I've supplied the cause. We wouldn't want dear Betty caught in a lie, now, would we?"

"I will have no arguments," said Suzanne, ushering them into the elevator. "We will need all our wits and strength tonight." She looked sharply at her middle sister. "That was not meant to be funny, Betty."

IX

Philippe Juneau's impeccable tailoring attracted attention in the lobby. Women of assorted heights and widths commented on it, and their men spent reluctant glances attempting to assess what the fuss was about. But it was more than the fit, the French styling of his blue pin-striped linen sports jacket, or the powder-blue silk shirt with the ruffled cuffs. It was a subdued charm and confidence reflected by his totality. The women absorbed the whole man and intuitively judged. The men saw a dandy, were puzzled, and changed the subject. Juneau wandered from the lobby to the bar, then out again. It was too early for him to drink. In an hour he would he the darling of the bartender, but not now. Digestion was the necessity of the moment, digestion and the psychological preparation that he had found requisite for an evening of fulfillment. The hotel had a library. Juneau had checked in advance, requesting pictures and a list of publications available there. Had the library not been to his satisfaction the conference would have been held at a hotel where it was. The lobby overflowed with lively guests anticipating the 10:30 dancing in the ballroom and the show that would follow. Philippe rightly judged that the library would be relatively unoccupied. He gathered the magazines he sought and placed them on the table next to a simulated leather armchair in a corner facing an unlit fireplace. His thoughts went back to ski lodges in Zermatt, St. Moritz, and Lucerne, where he had enjoyed the warmth of recovery from an exciting day on the slopes. He could never ski again as once he had, never savor the downhill thrills without an equal savoring of pain, never delight in the warmth of the lodge, but yearn instead for a frozen peak where the cold would numb his limbs and banish the pain. Even the medicine could not erase the consequences of a vigorous pursuit of a joy lost forever. He thumbed through the ski magazines first and at each color photo paused, remembering. The fashion magazines were next, and Juneau felt his ardor rising as he observed sketch after sketch and photo after photo of the manliness he had so carefully worked to epitomize. A laughing face coursed through his brain. It was a beautiful, curl-surrounded face, contorted by laughter. He snapped the magazine shut to squelch the sound. It had lasted three weeks one year ago, but sometimes he heard the laughter still. His thoughts went to his room and his king-size bed. There would be no laughter there tonight. He opened another magazine.

At 9:30 he went to the bar where, six drinks later but still sober, he had endeared himself to the bartender with his exceptional capacity for drink and an enormous tip. Adulation was the key to what mattered most to him, and with the key resting in his pocket he would find it. It was 9:45. He had told Nancy he would meet her after he had attended to some work that commanded his attention. He had entrusted her to George's keeping for the duration of the show, safe in the knowledge that George was undoubtedly the most reliable nursemaid in the world of social business, though that nursemaid had grumbled something about escorting his mother. Juneau was tickled at the thought. His entrance at 11:30 or thereabouts would be welcomed by all. He stepped out of the elevator and walked down the hall to his room. He opened the door and locked it behind him. Then he took a hanger and rapped three times on a chair. Two pieces of luggage at the foot of his bed stirred. The lids were lifted from within and out stepped two females. In the half-light of the room they looked very young. They wore gaily flowered smocks. One was brown-haired, the other blonde, and each had her hair in one enormous braid. They began undressing Juneau from behind, slowly, soundlessly. He closed his eyes. Despite their gentleness, the veins stood out on his forehead and neck and his lips were firmly compressed. He imagined the liquor sounding through his brain rather than the pain, as the metal corset stretching from his waist to his shoulders was unlatched. Freed of his crutch he slumped, but the girls caught him and laid him back upon the pillow. Sweat glistened on his face. The one with the dark hair lightly blotted his cheeks and forehead with a handkerchief. Then, in the dim light as Juneau watched, she slowly removed her smock and covered her nakedness with a gold, nylon gown that touched the floor. She loosened the ribbon on her braid and her hair cascaded down her back and around her face. She rocked over him, softly singing the songs of childhood, interspersing the lyrics with kisses on his ears, his chest, his thighs. She inserted a cloth ball in his mouth and stepped aside. Juneau's pale, lean body lay quietly as the blonde, now clad in black, her hair loose-flowing, drew near.

"You may dance with whom you like, but you are escorting me to the show."

"Mother, I promised Philippe to accompany Nancy Margot."

"And is a promise to your mother nothing? You won't have me forever, George."

"I'd prefer to escort you, of course, Mother. I certainly take babysitting with someone else's date as badly as the next man."

"The next man doesn't take it, you fool. You should have refused."

"I wasn't exactly asked."

"A man you haven't seen for years orders you to act the idiot and you agree. I advised you against associating with Philippe Juneau when you were a youngster, but apparently you are still not mature enough to take advice; you require an order. Well then, consider yourself ordered to escort me to the show. If you are to be under anyone's thumb it will be that of your mother, who at least loves you. Does Juneau love you? Does that slip of a Margot love you? Depend on it, George, no one loves as a mother loves. Miss Nancy Margot would do well to escort *her* mother to the show." And with a final sweep of her hand that disposed of all opposing arguments, she repeated with evident generosity, "You may dance with whom you like until 10:30. I shall watch." She brushed his face with a kiss and disappeared from the press of those on the rim of the dance floor.

George scanned the room for Nancy. He finally saw her dipping and twirling in the arms of someone who looked slightly familiar. He searched his brain for whom it was. Well, what did it matter. The man could not be counted on to relinquish Nancy after the show, though unless he were Philippe's equal at least, Nancy might eagerly relinquish him. His mother was wrong; he had learned a lot from advice. Then again the man's interest might extend only for the space of one dance, leaving Nancy with no escort to the show. Anyway, she was expecting him to escort her, wasn't she? George mopped his brow. Being single was hard work, even when you weren't working for yourself. It was foolish to intercept the dancers if the pleasant-looking young man were a substitute of whom Philippe would approve, but he couldn't be sure, his mother could not be denied, and something had to be done.

The young man stepped aside as George approached. "At 10:30 then," he said in parting.

"At 10:30?" said George, surprised. "But you were to allow me to escort you to the show tonight."

"I had no engagement with you for the show, George."

George silently cursed the propensity of some men to boast of conquests, but to ignore the inconvenient details of arranging them.

"Philippe asked me to escort you to the performance, and naturally I said yes. In the excitement he must have forgotten to tell you. I was anticipating it, but if you have already promised someone else, I must beg your pardon for interrupting your dance with the young man and offer my apology to Philippe, who was counting on my virtue in his absence."

Nancy was gleeful. "Oh, that was adorable, George. You're such a responsible person! But Philippe doesn't have to worry; I made it clear to Charles that my company doesn't extend beyond the night club this evening. I'm sorry if you're disappointed, but there's someone I think you'll find much more appealing company for the show. Suzanne has a tennis date at midnight, so if you like to turn in early she'll be no problem at all. But she's available for the show and she's super!"

George swallowed hard. Helping friends had its rewards after all. But his mother…From somewhere in the huge ballroom he was sure she was watching, probably with binoculars. "I hardly think your sister would care to—"

"Oh, but she would!"

"She would?" His heart filled with elation and despair "But if she doesn't know, that is if I haven't asked, what I mean is if she doesn't know that she would—"

"She'll know. Come with me and we'll ask her together." She took his hands.

"I couldn't. Really, this won't work."

"Of course it will work. I'll find her and ask her for you. She won't refuse someone she respects and admires."

"A flattering choice of words, but—"

"Those were Zanny's very words about you when she had no cause to exaggerate. I'll tell her and bring her back here so you two can have the last few dances together." She tripped gaily off, leaving George with a strong desire for the at least honest interchanges of the business meeting planned for tomorrow.

Now what was he to do? Unto others, that's what, using the popular interpretation of the text; he was desperate. He spotted Harry Bellemore dancing with Betty in the most crowded section of the room. For a man who preferred intimate corners this was unusual, but George was too absorbed in his own predicament to dwell on it. He hastened to Harry, begged the couple's pardon and, to the amazement of all, danced away with Harry.

"George, what are you doing? Are you mad?"

"Harry, you can't refuse me, you simply can't. We've been friends for years, and you know what friends are for."

"Get to the point, George. And stop dancing with me!" He wrenched his hands from George's.

"Philippe won't see Nancy until after the show and I promised to be with her until then. But I promised someone else as well, and the lady will not understand being abandoned to honor a commitment to another man. Harry, I know it's a sacrifice, but you do respect her nerve, you've said so. Do it for me, Harry; take her for me, Harry. She'll be furious at first, but with your charm, and the moonlight, and the madness…"

"George, George, get hold of yourself! Of course I'll help you; haven't I always?"

"It might be a bit awkward to escort both her and Betty," said George, somewhat ashamed and relenting.

"I haven't asked Betty for the show yet, so for your sake, George, I'll ignore her hints. She'll have no difficulty finding my replacement and I'll send her flowers in the morning."

"Harry, bless you! You're the only one whose company Leticia would enjoy. I'd rush to tell her the news myself, but coming from you it will be more the delightful surprise. At 10:30 outside the night club, if you don't catch sight of her before." George gave his friend a comradely hug and dashed off.

Harry stood there, amazed. Leticia! Clever George. Harry had taught him too well! Nancy Margot? Suzanne Margot was on the evening's agenda somewhere, Harry would swear to it. He shouldered his way to a table, sat down, and watched the whirl of events on the floor in a daze. A waiter hovered by his side.

"Scotch on the rocks." Leticia hated the smell of whisky. "Make it a triple."

George looked out into the lobby from the bank of house phones in the alcove. Phil was in the bushes for all he knew, but a call to his room was a sensible beginning and ending.

He had no intention of searching for his boyhood buddy beyond this attempt. Having informed or tried to inform him of Nancy's companion, he would have done his duty. George was about to replace the receiver when a barely audible voice reached his ear.

"Phil, it's George. It never occurred to me that you would be sleeping. Sometimes I forget what bedrooms are for. I just spoke to Nancy. She gives her word that she will meet you as planned, but she's already gotten a companion for the show. Nothing like the looks or sound of you, so you needn't worry."

There was a long silence. "Th-a-an-ks, Ge-orge."

"Phil, you sound ill. Phil? Phil!"

"I'm all-right-sleep-ing. La-ter Ge-orge."

"Phil!" But a click concluded the conversation. Sleepy? Drunk? Not that voice, not those sounds. George Crump moved quickly to the desk. With scruff imperatives he persuaded the night clerk to provide him with the second key to Juneau's room. He contemplated the stairs and only the timely arrival of the elevator saved him a run of seventeen flights.

He knocked on the door several times, at first gently, then with vigor, each time calling Phil's name. He fumbled with the key, inserted it in the lock and opened the door. The room was in total darkness, and George stood on the threshold blinking. He felt for the switch near the door and seconds later the room was bathed in light.

Philippe Juneau lay in bed, on either side of him a blonde and a brunette whose luxuriant hair flowed over the covers. George's face reddened and he began backing out of the room until his eyes fixed on Philippe. Between the amplitude of hair and curves Philippe looked very small, very pale, and very cadaverous. George entered and shut and locked the door.

"Get dressed and then get out." George pulled the blonde from the bed. Apart from the clasp of her hand in Philippe's, she offered no resistance. The brunette released Philippe's other hand, rose, and stood by the foot of the bed. Lascivious thoughts would have taken hold in George's head, but the scantily clad beauties and their allure were banished by Philippe's ghastly face. The recumbent man moved his head in a barely perceptible nod to the women, who removed themselves to the corners of the room to shed their gold and black and reclaim their flowered smocks.

"I'm calling a doctor."

"No, no, Ge-orge, Please."

"He will not be sitting up for another hour," explained the brunette. "He has only just taken his medicine. Then he will feel fine, a little tired, but fine. His recovery will be rapid after that."

"We cannot leave, but we will adjourn to the lavatory if you would like to sit alone with him," suggested the blonde.

George looked at Phil, but he had closed his eyes and effectively forestalled questioning.

"You must tell me what's wrong with him."

The two women said nothing.

George spotted the metal contraption on the armchair. He walked to it, lifted it, and wordlessly put it down. "Poor Phil," he muttered. "So that's it. And for so many years, such unnecessary torture. Can anything be worth such pain?"

The figure stirred slightly in the bed. "Yes," he said.

George sat with Philippe the hour. He would not hear of leaving, although the women assured him that they were capable of attending him. So George Crump sat by his friend's bed and thought about Philippe's pain, and tried to recall when last he had sought pain, and what kind, and for what reason. He concluded sadly that he had wanted nothing badly enough to risk great pain.

"You should not be alone this evening."

George was jolted out of his reverie. "Phil, what a relief to hear your voice!"

Philippe managed a smile. The color was returning to his face. "I would have been pleased to sound more normal for you, George, if I had been forewarned of your phone call and arrival. Go downstairs and busy yourself this evening as I shall. We two were meant for marriage. It's an end to emotional insecurity and loneliness, an end to having to hack it alone psychologically. As you see, I manage, but marriage, well conceived, is better."

"Derek seems happy enough without it, and Harry is so doggedly opposed to it that his happiness gets no consideration at all. But once one overcomes the fright of getting married, there is the fright of choosing unwisely. When will you get it right, Phil?"

Phil gave a shallow laugh with his returning strength. "Maybe next time, if you will help me."

"I can't think of anyone for you right off, but I'll work on it. Mother knows a lot of people. I could finagle some names out of her."

"Horrors, no, George. Selecting a mate is a very personal business. Neither you nor Leticia could get inside may head to make that choice, and lucky too; my mind is crowded enough. Help me sit up, George. The fact is that I have a potential Madame Juneau waiting for me tonight."

"Nancy Margot! But you've only met her. Quick decisions are anathema to marriage."

"So are those that never reach fruition. George, George, a man has to take a stand, take a chance, and hope for the best."

"On what do you base the hope that you have found the ideal wife?"

"On an open, unsophisticated mind and an eagerness to please. Nancy Margot is the type of woman to best appreciate a man of the world who is intelligent and adoring."

"That would be you, I presume."

Phil's laugh was stronger now. "That *could* be me."

"And what if, following your example, she becomes secretive, knowledgeable, and eager to *be* pleased? What becomes of your happy marriage, then?"

"And what if I'm struck by a meteor."

"If you are, you may lose more than the enormous sum your last wife carted off, no doubt in return for silence about a piece of steel. You're being foolish again, Phil." He frowned at the wall. "But what did you have in mind?"

"George, you are so flexible, you would make a wonderful husband. As you may have seen, sensed, and concluded, the older sister is the boss. Her approval is mandatory in matters of coupling. You have established a rapport with her. I'm sure she is, once you get to know her, as sensible and flexible as yourself, and since it is her obvious aim to have her sisters well matched, and since after the faux pas of Betty this may be more difficult to do, I think she might appreciate the title of sister-in-law to Philippe Juneau. Could you manage to make her better acquaintance and speak well of your old college chum?"

"I'm escorting her to the show tonight. I've gotten Harry to take Mother."

Phil's eyebrows rose. "A definite coup; congratulations. But you had better go now; it's nearly 10:30. I'll be fine and if I should swoon, I've got four hands to hold me that are infinitely prettier than yours."

"The Margots are ordinary people with a twist of lemon. Aren't you afraid of marrying into such a family?"

"A synthesis of both my families! See you later, George."

"If you don't, I'm coming up to check on you." He patted the covers and walked to the door.

Juneau fell back upon the pillow. "Definitely a product of Leticia," he said.

X

Nancy waved vigorously to George in the lobby. "With that crush in the ballroom I couldn't find you again. Zanny says she doesn't want to impose on you; she was unconvincible. I had to reserve a family table—I didn't tell her about Charles—but," she said conspiratorially, "I made the reservation in your name. Table 21, up front."

"I wouldn't want your sister to feel uncomfortable," began George uncomfortably.

"Oh, it's just the unexpectedness of it all. Zanny isn't used to having things done for her. She sees me all the time anyway, but you're special. Ah, there's Charles. Have a good evening, Mr. Crump," she said pumping his hand, and she was gone.

George Crump would have liked to find out what made him special, feeling imminent need of a bolstered ego, but he gathered what courage he had and proceeded to table 21.

"Miss Margot, your sister has been appropriated by a young man, one Charles. May I sit down?"

"Mr. Crump, I must apologize for my sister. Forcing you into this situation was both rude and inconsiderate."

"Earlier you apologized to me for Betty's behavior, do you remember? Are there any other apologies you wish to dispense, or may we get on with enjoying ourselves?"

"I'm sorry, Mr. Crump."

"Another apology!"

They both laughed. "I can't seem to stop, can I?"

"I hear we're in for an evening of music, magic, and acrobatics. If at any time you weary of it, we can adjourn for some fresh air." He smiled.

"Do you remember when we last met on a walk in the woods?"

"Must we speak of that disconcerting experience?"

"I'm naturally curious about what changed your antipathy toward me."

"Your apologies!"

"I still have those notes," she teased, "but they seem to have had no effect on Mr. Bellemore."

"I never told him about them. I rarely act in haste, so I was willing to wait and see what further action you took. In my admiration for your conduct since, I forgot about their existence."

Suzanne was aware of his kindness in saying so and George was aware of his kindness in saying so. Both suddenly felt remarkably comfortable with the other, as brother and sister might, despite the waiting moon, stars, or whatever actually was overhead.

"Abandoned by my own son. If George Sr. were alive he would die of embarrassment."

"Fortunately, you are a hardier soul."

"You're making fun of me, Harry, and I won't tolerate it. I did not ask for your company this evening. I asked for my son's."

"Adopt me."

"Which girl has he an eye for this time?"

"This time? You've confused George with me already! Have pity, the man's entitled to date girls occasionally without your permission."

The old lady pointed to herself. "Not when this girl here is a guest."

Bellemore leaned over and whispered in her ear. "And who asked you to be, Leticia dear?"

"You are discreetly rude, as usual, Harry."

"Would you like a drink?"

"Yes," she said maliciously, "Lafite-Rothschild"

"The sign says no wine is served in the night club," he said sweetly.

"And you know I drink nothing more potent, dear," she answered with equal sugar. "Lafite-Rothschild. Waiter!"

"Leticia, please; you are being difficult."

"George is being difficult, you are being difficult and I am merely requesting Lafite-Rothschild. If you persist in provoking me, the year—"

"All right, all right. Lafite-Rothschild for my darling. I'll invade the bar and bring it to you myself."

Harry Bellemore surveyed the night club as he walked briskly to the exit. Finding one woman among several hundred people under dim lights would have been a bolt of luck, and luck was not to make its appearance at that moment, or the moment following, for that matter. He had sent the bartender in search of the wine when a voice over his shoulder sent his brain into preliminary calisthenics.

"How quickly one forgets one's friends. Or are you ashamed to be seen with me?"

"Betty, of course not. I meant to wish you a good evening and to thank you for the pleasure of dancing with you." His voice was steady, clear, and formal.

"You disgust me" she spat, and turned to go.

He grabbed her upper arm. "Just a moment. Perhaps you would like to join us for the show. You and my companion are not strangers."

"I am violently opposed to that kind of sharing." She wrenched her arm from his.

"I rather think the old woman is too," he said evenly.

Betty turned on him. "You mean you're with her?'"

Harry hung his head and murmured the softest "yes."

"Oh, Harry, what have I done? Placating that old witch for me! How brave and wonderful of you! I deserve to be alone."

"I'll understand if you make some young man fortunate here tonight. I don't mean to be selfish, but if after the show—"

"Selfish? Oh, you are galaxies away from selfishness, and I wouldn't dream of looking elsewhere for companionship tonight." It was clear to them both that she had looked, but except for several leering drunks, in vain.

"You may wish to sit with Nancy, then, or the Mother Hen."

Betty giggled. "That's for sure. A twosome is preferable to you and whats-her-name, even if number two is Zanny."

Then Suzanne Margot was alone for the evening. "May I escort you to your table?"

"It's number 21, I think."

"Let's make sure." And Harry Bellemore took the Lafite in one hand and Betty by the other and returned to the night club. An inquiry yielded no reservation for Margot and it was only Betty, in panic at the thought that her older sister had gotten, however temporarily, a man, and all but dragging Bellemore from the cadre at the entrance, who prevented him from reserving a private table for the lady herself. Had Bellemore been in his usual truthful spirit, he would have inwardly admitted to a pang of panic himself. Determination and speed brought Betty and Bellemore, flexing squashed fingers, to the desired table.

"I hate to intrude," said Betty, pulling a chair from an adjacent table. But the couple there rebelled and Betty was forced to relinquish it. "I'm sure I'm not welcome, anyway." Protests galore.

Bellemore motioned to the waiter. "A chair for the young lady." He hoped he was assuming a paternal air. "I'm glad you found your Margot, George, though I thought it was to be Nancy." He stole a quick look at Suzanne. No remorse, no shock, no anger.

"Is the wine your gift for being unable to stay?"

Harry answered so smoothly that no one within hearing would have guessed he badly wanted to lay one on George's chin. "No, I dare not disappoint a charming lady who is expecting her Lafite-Rothschild."

"Oh, yes, yes, of course," stammered George. "That's very good of you."

"Good evening, Mr. Bellemore."

Her voice changed his heartbeat. He had thrown etiquette to the devil and ignored her very existence! "Good evening, Miss Margot. Ladies, George, a good evening to you all."

George stirred in his seat and gazed after Harry with some concern. "That wasn't like Harry at all. He's always been the gentleman, in public at least."

"He's undoubtedly anxious to return to his lady," Suzanne stated.

"That old hag?"

"Betty, really!"

"Well, that's what she is—an ancient lady with a mouthful of rotting teeth."

George cleared his throat. "Actually, they're not rotting, and only a few are missing. That's—that's Mother."

"His mother! Good Lord, Zanny, you might at least have told me I'd be gambling with his mother! I hope I didn't say too many nasty things about her. No wonder he was so cool. It's your fault!"

"Shush, lower your voice. What are you talking about?"

"The old lady at the pool, the one you wanted me to play back-gammon with—she's a professional gambler. I wound up owing her $225, but Harry got me out of it. He—why that louse! He wanted me to feel obligated, grateful—"

"Betty, you will speak like a lady or leave the table this instant!"

"It's hard to speak like a lady when you're not talking about a gentleman," she responded morosely. "He knew I would have to enter the beauty contest because he wanted me to. Some big-deal hero! And it's your fault too; you should have known where it would all lead. You deserved to be embarrassed."

Even in the dim light George could see that Suzanne had become pale. He urged the remaining martini on her, but she waved it away.

"I didn't know she was his mother or that she gambled. I'm sorry."

"Well," said Betty relenting, "she's probably not such a bad old lady. He probably put her up to it. What a man will do to get a woman!"

Any bud of warmth Suzanne had felt for Harry Bellemore froze. He had fallen into the bottomless abyss of her judgment. The possibility that this—this person might feel for Betty what he had never felt for any other woman became remote. And perhaps it was best. She owed her sister counsel that would lead to her happiness, and the character of Harry Bellemore did not seem designed with provision for that. She had not questioned her mother's goals in years. She was questioning them now.

George drank his vodka ferociously, nearly biting the glass. He had done his friend a disservice and was continuing to do so. He had allowed Harry to be maligned without correction and saddled him with a second mother, a fine reward for his freeing George for the night. And his mother had been gambling again. She was an impossible woman, but no mother of his was an old hag. She had always been a doting, if difficult, mother. He cleared his throat; it was not too late to speak.

Betty laughed suddenly, and then again, until gales of laughter crescendoed from her mouth. "Can you imagine," she finally managed to say, "Don Juan coming to a hotel with his mother?"

George Crump closed his mouth and finished his vodka.

Her binoculars caught Harry's return, and Leticia Candleby Crump tucked her spare eyes into her purse. "Thank you, Harry dear. I will be no further bother to you. No," she moved her fingers to her lips to stifle the impending denial, "I know when I've been a bother, when George has deserted me, and when I am thirsty." She sipped the Lafite. "You have missed choice entertainment, the sickening, simpering banality of it all—a crasher repulsed, polite formality coupled with devastating crust. The stage performance will be anticlimax. I'm going to bed." She sipped the wine again. "That will give you a table for two. Is it too late to manage my replacement?"

"If you're leaving because—"

"I'm not leaving to do you any favor; you know me better than that. I need my sleep. But if you haven't the courage to fill my seat with more than wrinkled skin and white hair, then I'll force myself to stay awake."

Harry Bellemore looked into the faded eyes. "Well shot, old psychic. I wouldn't admit it to anyone else."

Leticia hailed the waiter. "A double scotch, here."

"I've already had too much, and it won't help."

"Tip the man, Harry," she ordered unnecessarily. "Love is incapacitating. You have my sympathy and my double scotch. You want the oldest one, I suppose."

"You don't miss anything."

"I can't afford to miss anything where George is concerned, and your future has a bearing on his. It's his mid-life crisis, I gather, not totally unexpected, but worrisome nonetheless. I'm willing to allow George some fun as long as he doesn't do anything rash."

"Like run away from one of his homes and get married."

"A strong woman will make a rug out of him, and a weak one will not give him the support he needs. Yet, much as I rebel at the thought, he will have to marry some day; there is no guarantee I will get permission to guide him from on high. I rather counted on you, Harry."

"Isn't George too old for me?"

"Nothing like a double scotch—for men. Now that your faculties are in order again, I confess I like the idea of sisters, but not this particular set. Sisters have been dwelling on the lower level of my mind for some time. The Wingate sisters so rich, so charming, so like the dear dowager, but married for years, naturally; the good ones go fast. The Van Fortin women—sparkling Alice is on the verge of divorce, entre nous, of course. You used to fancy Alice, and Mildred would be a soothing companion for George. She only admits to forty-one. And then there are the Windmere girls, gigglers the lot, but they are young, and with proper training. What I'm saying, Harry, is that I should like nothing better than to have you and George brothers-in-law. Then I can die in peace."

"You underestimate your son. George can make it on his own. We all can, if we have to. But you're willing to accept the Misses Margot?"

Leticia sighed heavily. "I'd rather not, Harry. I checked, but it's obvious. They're nothing, you know. No money, rank, nothing but pretty faces, working girls with a widowed mother who keeps them traipsing around the country, and for all I know the world, looking for wealthy husbands. Mind you, I'm not against the poor improving their lot, but that doesn't mean I thrill at the prospect of sacrificing George for their success. And that middle one—a trial to any mother. Naturally she's out of the question for George. I'm not sure even marriage would change a creature like that. It's a matter of character, Harry. Toying with her as you have done—and in the most gallant fashion too, I must add—is one thing, but calling her family." She shuddered. "She has the makings of a slut. Are you sure it's love you feel and not sunstroke?"

"I don't know. I think of her at the oddest times. I want to do things for her, take care of her, argue with her, shake her."

"Smother her with kisses, clasp her to your bosom, and fly with her to Venus despite her objections that you've both got busy schedules and the railroad would prove more economical." The warmth of memory lit her face. "But she will learn quickly. I did.

Well then, if there is nothing for it, you had best disengage her from my son and find someone else for that snippet—don't you dare leave her with George. I can find my way back to my room alone, thank you."

"I don't think disengagement will sit well with either George or Suzanne."

"Cowed! Heavens, you are serious. You've been so good at thinking of women as mere women. That's the way it should be before marriage. If men think of them as equals they are not likely to succeed in persuading them to enter into matrimony at all. As for George, he doesn't know his own mind, never has. The youngest sister seems malleable. With a little training—Go find her and bring her to George."

"She's with the desk clerk."

Leticia cast her eyes toward the ceiling. "Her mother will see stars. But it shows modesty, moderation. With a little training, her taste—"

"Leticia, I can't reorder people's emotions or lives."

"No one is asking you to. But what do you know of their feelings, their needs? You know only of yours. To the game, man! You'll find out whether your advances are welcome or not. If I gaze intensely at your face while we speak or grip your arm while we walk, it may mean nothing more than that I left my contact lenses in my room— if I were young and pretty and if I wore contact lenses, that is. Then again, it may reflect Olympian passions. A real man would find out!"

"God bless you, Leticia, but I can't hurt George."

"You're a coward, Harry Bellemore. Such talk is not the talk of a man in love. Ah, there go the lights. I will stay up with you after all. If that doesn't drive you to your alleged love I can't imagine what will."

Betty stated her opinions clearly, loudly, and frequently. If anyone doubted her importance at the table, this underscoring of her presence surely dispelled it. If her views that ballroom dancing was passé, acrobats belonged at the circus, and magicians were child fare were shared by her tablemates, they did not venture to record them. Betty felt blissfully in charge, as was so necessary when she felt devoid of bliss itself. Harry was a man and his tricks forgivable if the drama concluded with her assuming the role of Mrs. Bellemore. And of this she was not completely sure. She raised her voice again.

"It's all so dull, Zanny. Must we stay?"

"Of course not, dear. Just make sure you leave the chain unlatched so I can unlock the door."

Betty stared sullenly at the stage. Suzanne smiled inwardly, a brief smile, a half smile, a painful smile. She understood her sister well, but she did not understand Harry Bellemore well, at least not well enough to know whether he had abandoned Betty or was merely playing lost lover. A review of the totality of his behavior toward Betty had reignited hope in the latter possibility. He was detestable, but he could control Betty and amuse her, and that was important. Her personal feelings about him had no bearing on the match, but his mother was an important new element to consider. Suzanne had no illusions about the impression Betty made on women. The gambling incident and the beauty contest fiasco had functioned as tests, and even in school Betty had done poorly in those. The more she thought of it, the more Suzanne was sure that Mrs. Bellemore held the key to her son's success with Betty and Betty's success in winning him. She resolved to address herself to that key and manipulate it, if necessary. Her mother, she knew, would do no less.

Suzanne lingered over the applause, waiting for Mrs. Bellemore, as she supposed, to rise. Then she did likewise and, urging Betty and George to remain seated, followed her quarry and Bellemore to the exit. In the lobby Bellemore strode idly, hands in pockets, as his senior ambled to the Powder Room. Suzanne hesitated. The entrance was glutted, and that sanctuary seemed hardly a suitable setting for such conversation as she had in mind. Still, it might afford a reasonable excuse for introductions, at least. But she had hesitated too long, and Barry Bellemore was upon her before she could effect her plan.

"Did you enjoy the show?"

How banal, how trite, she thought. "Yes, and you?"

She's making this difficult, he thought. "I did."

"If you'll excuse me."

"Is Betty with George?"

"Yes, he's guarding her for you. That status quo may not last." She resisted adding that Betty might depart in disgust at any moment and let her implication stand. "You'd do well to hurry."

"That's thoughtful of friend George, but he can relax and enjoy her company. I'm not selfish."

"You mean you're not possessive," corrected Suzanne.

"I *am* possessive. I mean I'm not selfish. The devil, do you think I *am* selfish? Have I acted selfishly toward you?"

"I did not say that you were selfish, but an unselfish willingness to share a woman implies a casual interest in that woman which unpossessiveness does not"

"My choice of word was fitting for my purpose."

"I am very sorry to hear that, Mr. Bellemore. Has any of your behavior in the past few days been of a serious nature?"

"All my pursuits are serious, and if you insist on trivializing and personalizing them then I must say you have a meager understanding of my character."

"So you believe you have character, Mr. Bellemore?"

"I take it you are implying that a man of character would marry your sister."

Blind fury robed in sibling loyalty and righteousness attacked her senses. "A man of character would be honored to marry a woman of such charm, vivaciousness, and devotion as my sister."

"I have no aversion to the name Margot. In fact, I've grown to have a special feeling for it. You have shown some sensibility of my affection for it, and if we can dispense with semantics I hope to persuade you of both my seriousness and my character, but since you seem intent on arguing, may I suggest that we remove ourselves to private quarters before I satisfy your demands and dissolve your outrage?"

"A constructive idea, Mr. Bellemore. Where do you suggest?"

"My room, perhaps?"

A sharp pain bit into his cheek. "You have an antediluvian sense of humor," he responded coldly.

"To pair with your sense of gallantry." She turned abruptly from him, her brain teeming with indignation. She stormed into the nearest refuge from his effrontery. The crush of patrons in the Powder Room keenly etched reality before her and brought her face to face with the woman to whom she could now think of nothing rational to say.

"Are you all right, my dear?"

"Yes, yes, thank you," she said, attempting to suppress her bewilderment.

"You look frightful. Will one of you young ladies get up," she addressed a group of middle-aged matrons. "This woman is ill."

"I'm fine, really. No, ladies, please don't bother." But they had already risen, and despite her mortification she sank gratefully into the cushions of the couch.

The old lady demanded wet hand towels and they were forthcoming with speed. "Calm yourself; good, good. The color is returning to your cheeks."

Suzanne blushed more desperately. Her mind raced. Harry Bellemore's mother would report this weakness. How he would laugh at it! She would have to set the matter right immediately, but she despised liars. She would not lie.

"My mother's telegram—her debilitation—no hope—insists we enjoy ourselves." She gasped out the words, not from a sense of drama, but from a sense of something akin to shame. The result was the same.

"How awful for you, my dear. What is she suffering from?"

But all Suzanne could do was shake her head in speechless stupor and rise. She exhaled audibly. "Thank you, but you must excuse me. I'm quite all right now."

Harry Bellemore was waiting outside the door. "I insist on being heard, and if you have even a scrap of fairness in that rebellious body of yours you will listen to me."

The sound of the louder, emotion-charged passages of *Goyescas* took over her mind. They blotted out the voice of Harry Bellemore and imbued her with the determination and speed necessary to get her to her room. She glanced at him once or twice—as they descended the lobby steps, in the elevator. His face was impassioned, his words possibly eloquent, the passion of flattery and persuasion. *Goyescas* reached a deafening level. She emerged from the elevator, Bellemore still at her side, oblivious of other passengers, other guests, talking, talking. She unlocked the door to the Margot suite and quickly shut it in his face.

Harry Bellemore stood there, stunned, stunned and furious. He had proposed marriage and she had not even deigned a reply. Her gall, her insolence were monumental! How had he presumed to pay his addresses to someone so beneath him? He ignored the elevator and took the stairs two at a time to the lobby and the outdoors. The warm air fed the maelstrom within him and he fled the hotel at a brisk clip, oblivious of the strolling couples, the distant music, and the moonlit grounds.

XI

Suzanne faced with surprise and pleasure the woman in their suite.

"It seems we have more than one perplexing situation to deal with. Good; I would hate to know I left the comfort of our home for some inconsequential nonsense. When Betty screams 'foul' one never knows. Sit down, darling. I didn't expect to see you until morning, but in such matters delay prolongs the anguish. Not so in bridge; I have every hope that absence will make Sir Luck fonder of me than he has been of late. I see you got my telegram."

She held up the paper that had arrived that afternoon. Suzanne remembered it clearly: "Debilitation continues. My bridge a shambles. No hope unless you send cheering news."

"Oh, Mother, I'm not any good at this." She wrung her hands in despair.

"Betty phoned me with a jumbled account of a debacle at the pool this morning. Mulling it over saved me the price of a romantic novel on the flight down. Here, have some of this warm milk; it will soothe you. Now, the facts about this morning, darling."

"Mother, I just did something awful. What's become of my pride, my self-respect?"

"Oh dearest, this *does* sound promising, but if you begin with Betty's drama you won't feel quite as shaken when you arrive at yours." She put her arm around her daughter's shoulders. "There, there, I know it's important; you look ghastly. Half the glass of milk before you utter another word. Very good. Now, the saga of Betty." Mrs. Margot allowed her daughter to speak without interruption. One of the pleasures of listening to her eldest was her certainty of hearing thorough yet concise explanations, complete with ramifications, potential and real.

"He would be defiant for sheer enjoyment if he weren't serious about Betty. Instead he's acted the thoughtful, gallant confidant with me. Yet he denies the desire to have her to himself. There is no sense to it, unless his mother balked at making Betty a Bellemore and persuaded the son. What else but guilt would cause him to follow me to our suite with useless excuses and apologies, and what does it matter if the bottom line is rejection?"

"Promising indeed. Very! But I rather wish you had listened to those apologies and excuses in your usual meticulous manner, dear. As for old Mrs. Bellemore, she has been dead these ten years."

"But George said—"

"Yes, George said. And why do you think he said?"

"To discredit his best friend? I can't believe that."

"And you shouldn't. George Crump was making an extemporaneous effort to prevent casting discredit on himself. The socially insecure are very sensitive to thoughtless implications concerning apron strings. Betty made one, and for all Mr. Crump knew you had silently made one too. Since he chose to sit with you, at some pains I might add, and since you got on well, he naturally had no wish to have his masculinity impugned."

"Why do you say he went to great pains?"

"Because by right he should have been sitting with his mother. How he palmed her off on Harry Bellemore must have been, for him, sheer inspiration. Leticia Candleby Crump does not take kindly to being traded, and Mr. Bellemore is not easily dissuaded from pursuing choice objects."

"Mother, what are you talking about?"

"I'm talking about you, darling. Harry Bellemore is mad about *you*. Dropping Mrs. Crump—there will be hell to pay for that— walking you to this room with a constant stream of what looked like 'impassioned' chatter—your word, dear—in the face of your obvious disgust. How I *wish* you had listened to him. Dear Suzanne, you have made two conquests, hardly what I expected, but delightful all the same." She kissed her daughter. "Betty will have to switch her affections to Derek Barnesforth. It won't be a good match from the standpoint of longevity, but perhaps I'll be surprised. My mind had appropriated Mr. Barnesforth or Mr. Juneau for Nancy, but since Philippe and Nancy have paired off we will have to give Betty and Derek a try. There is no sense wasting a good man."

"Mother, I do not want to get married now, and Mr. Bellemore is not in love with me. He is Betty's choice. She was, at least once, his, and they are going to have each other. I can see to that and, if necessary, I *will* see to that."

"You're too excited dear."

"I'm not excited. They belong together. It will be a good marriage, a lasting marriage, but above all, a marriage. That is what we want, isn't it?"

Mrs. Margot handed her daughter the glass. "Finish the milk, dear, and I suggest you go straight to bed."

"I can't. I've got a midnight tennis appointment with Mr. Barnesforth."

"Really, Suzanne! This is quite unlike you. How can you be so mean-spirited to take all the men when your sisters are in need?"

Suzanne laughed and her mother joined her. "Quite unlike! The result of some unfathomable, grotesque magic and in no way of my doing. I'm the pawn in some game being played by the company of Bellemore, Crump, and Barnesforth, and it will all amount to nothing. I would be a fool to expect otherwise. I don't seriously believe that you do."

"Love is never pragmatic. I should know. Did I marry your father for his money? I did not. Did I want to marry money? I did. I believed his preposterous stories of wealth partially because I was naive, but mainly because I wanted to believe them. It is quite conceivable to me that the games of our wealthy quartet may ultimately prove not to be games at all, even if that was their original intent, or the games of one or two, rather than all four. Dearest, if you anticipate rejection you invite it."

"I'm being realistic, Mother," she averred stubbornly.

"Let's hope not, dear."

"Oh, Mother, look at me!" She stood in front of a full-length mirror. "Is this a vision to swoon over? I have mousy hair, a thin face, and dull gray eyes. I'm shapelessly thin and I've no charm at all."

"You hardly sound worth playing games with! But no daughter of mine fits the description you have just given. I see before me an attractive and charming young woman."

"Oh, Mother, you are blinded by love."

Mrs. Margot smiled. "If so, remember that three men may be also. Now, are Betty and Nancy spoken for tonight?"

"Betty has no one, unless she seeks out Harry Bellemore and attaches herself to him; we know she's capable of doing that. I doubt if she's still with George Crump; she's said he has a horse-and-buggy mentality, and he's hardly the dashing Romeo she likes. Nancy has a date with Juneau after the show. I—I wish it were with Barnesforth. Something about Juneau bothers me. His manner is too—I've been trying to find the right word—too contained, too unnatural, too something. I've rechecked the clippings and spoken to the man, but I still can't place what's wrong, only that something is. He told me that his flawless posture is the result of a bad back acquired in a skiing accident, but that doesn't explain an unsettling something about him. If he has some private trouble, all the money in the world may not make marriage with him worthwhile."

"Have you mentioned this to Nancy?"

"No."

"Listen, dear, you have half an hour before your tennis date. You must go downstairs, find Betty, and settle her with someone handsome for the evening. Betty alone when her sisters are not equals trouble. One faux pas from her per hunting expedition is enough. I will reexamine the clippings on Juneau while you are gone. You may whisper my presence to Betty. That may carry her through the night on acceptable behavior, date or no date."

Ordinarily Suzanne would have felt comfortable in the lobby and ballroom scenes. The anonymity of the crowds would have enabled her to indulge in her favorite hobby, observing human nature at work, while enjoying the music, the commotion, the hubbub in playful and relaxed spirits. This was not now the case, for Betty was nowhere to be found, Nancy was nowhere to be seen, and Harry and George, if present, had become invisible.

The uncertainty of events in progress filled her with uneasiness. Even Leticia Candleby Crump had disappeared. The woods were dark and the rooms were many. She shivered. A check of the coffee shop and cocktail lounge proved futile. There was nothing to do but to change for her part in this charade.

The tennis courts were bordered by a swaying darkness, some frilly edges of which were illumined by the court lights looming almost the height of some of the surrounding trees. Derek Barnesforth was waiting under a court light, a straw basket by his side.

"I'm glad you came; I wasn't sure you would."

"I always keep my word." She removed the racket from its cover.

"Always this reluctantly?"

"Stand-offishness is part of my nature. You mustn't take it personally."

"I'll try to remember that. I hope you won't object if I create the balance to it. It may be nothing more than shedding a few tears if you defeat me, but I can't promise that will be the extent of it."

"I'll understand," she said, beginning to cross to her court.

"Even under a full moon?" He waved his racket at the sky.

Suzanne, well behind the base line, waved her readiness at Derek.

"Warm-up," he shouted, and applied a powerful smash to the object in his hand sending it careening across the net. As it wobbled toward her Suzanne allowed it to fall and lowered her racket. Derek was at the net now emitting a bird call and smiling broadly. Images of college badminton fluttered through her mind as she picked up the plastic bird and read the note attached: "Champagne warm-up at the net." She marched to meet Derek.

"After the game in celebration, not before," she said.

"If I lose I may not want to celebrate. Isn't the fact that you've come celebration enough?"

"Not for me, but just a taste to make you happy."

"Would that I were so easily made happy, but it's a start." The picnic basket yielded two glasses and a half bottle of Krug. They sat on a bench half-bathed in darkness, clinked glasses, and sipped the champagne.

Derek smiled.

"Pity I didn't bring canvas and paint. With a palette knife I could bring a jungle lushness to life with a creep of foliage that will not be denied impinging on static green."

"Improvise. Earth is freely available and mixed with champagne will make a usable medium. Your shirt stretched between four rocks can be canvas, blades of grass and your fingers the brushes. Your imagination can change the brown to green and you will have captured a memorable night."

"Will you help make it memorable?"

"I'll help you place the four rocks."

He uttered a boyish laugh. "How would you paint the scene?"

"In the style of Watteau, with vanishing paint."

"So this moment is uncapturable, you think?"

"Uncapturable if we sat here forever. Like people. Like this particular tennis game which is slipping away in painted dreams." She rose. His eyes were clouded and sad and she was half sorry she had spoken, but Nancy would appeal more, and it was to Nancy that he must speak of foliage and art and dreams. "Warm-up," she said. "Really," and crossed to her court again.

As usual, Suzanne found the sound of ball on racket restful, and mingled with the call of crickets enveloped in the darkness especially pleasing. Yet she was not tired, despite the hour. The contrast of dark and light and the moving figure beyond the net kept her alert and invigorated. "Good shot," "beautiful," "right down the middle." They alternated encouragement. Overhead in all its fullness, the moon shone, possibly accounting for the seeming interest of three men in her and for Betty's morning behavior, she thought, as she reached for a backhand. But the day was nearly over, and with it the foolishness. No matter if Betty had gone off somewhere and if Nancy were with Philippe. Mother had arrived, and the day was nearly over.

She smartly returned a wicked serve. If only she could play tennis forever.

"Your set! Intermission!" Derek sheathed his racket and waited for her at the bench. "You certainly give a guy a workout on the court. I'll bet you're even—"

"—better off the court."

"My lines are that bad, huh?"

"Familiar."

"I hope the remainder of this picnic basket redeems me from predictability. I'll bet you the next set you can't guess."

Suzanne thought of Betty and Leticia Crump and vigorously shook her head. "You can win the set fairly, I'm sure."

"I'm beginning to doubt my ability to win anything this night." And so saying he removed the contents of the basket. On the bench between them he placed two boxes of Animal Crackers and the Krug. On his lap he placed a recorder, its burnished mahogany length shining under the lamplight. "I couldn't fit a piano in," he explained.

Suzanne clasped her hands together in delight. Animal Crackers had been her childhood favorite, and the same funny, little creatures gazed at her from the cover of the circus box. The recorder conjured up pictures of Elizabethan England, Shakespeare's plays, and the courses in medieval literature she had enjoyed so much.

Derek was gratified, for although Suzanne had said nothing, her pleasure was evident.

"No male chauvinist, I. You have the choice of serving the champagne and cookies or playing a few medieval ditties on the wood."

She grabbed the recorder, bopped him playfully on the head with it and handed it back to him. She poured the wine into glasses she sat on the lid of the basket and then arranged the crackers on the brown-swirled pottery plate. The camel led the circular parade, followed by the giraffe, the zebra, and the other independents. The cat family brought up the rear. All the while Derek played, and when she had finished and looked up at him he began to sing. His soft voice caressed the lyrics and seemed to float effortlessly from him. The plights of the banished swain and the lovesick knight fell from his lips with such grace and poignancy that Suzanne was moved. He caught the signs and cleverly concluded with a formal song of courtly love, discreet, subdued. Suzanne applauded his voice, his playing, his finesse, his diplomacy, his directness, and his undeniable charm.

"How lovely," she breathed. "I'm afraid you've charmed me out of the will to win our last set."

"That was only partially the idea." He picked up a camel.

They nibbled the crackers, sipped the wine, and spoke of magic—the magic of Paris at night, of London at midday, and of Venice at all times. Suzanne asked and Derek answered. Yes, he had been to Morocco and ridden a real camel. The ones on the crackers were more amusing and more comfortable. A breeze blew by them and Suzanne stirred. The crackers were gone and the Krug was empty.

"What time is it? I think we've talked away the night!"

"In the most delightful way. It's 2 A.M. We can go inside, if you like and call the game a draw."

Suzanne forced her mind back from the places to which their conversation and her fancy had taken it. She wanted nothing more at this moment than to get into her own bed and continue the pleasant fantasy of the past hour, but she knew this must not be. "I wouldn't want this game to rankle in memory as incomplete, and neither should you. You've mesmerized me so with songs and stories that I'm sure I won't even make a decent showing in this set."

But make a decent showing she did, as she knew she would, as she knew she must. Reluctantly, she realized she would have to win. The real Derek Barnesforth was a dreaming puppy. He could afford to keep reality in its place—far away from him, but she could not. He was an excellent player and would not take kindly to losing, which was why he had to lose. And he did.

"Nancy will envy me this lovely time with you. Unfortunately, she's not a particularly good tennis player."

A downcast Derek Barnesforth raised his eyes to hers at this, and the sparkle of the castle-builder and little boy began to revive.

Suzanne stopped short. Controlled. That was the word she had been seeking to describe Philippe Juneau. Debonair, continental, erect, but above all controlled. She began walking faster and Derek hurried to catch up with her. For both the magic of the night was over. Images crowded her mind, all the strange faces somehow familiar, *someone* familiar. Her thoughts darted back through the rooms and corridors of the hotel to the flight they had taken, and suddenly there she was—the brunette reading the magazine an aisle away. The same flight, the same airport destination, the same girl in the background of a Juneau clipping of several years before.

"Are you all right?"

"Fine, just a little tired. That tennis victory came hard. Thank you for a thoroughly agreeable time." And she walked the remaining steps to the hotel with speed that belied her words.

"May I see you to your room?" said Derek Barnesforth to the air. He shrugged and entered the hotel.

It was 2 A.M. Where were Nancy and Betty? She dialed a house phone in the lobby to find out. Her mother answered and both voice and news were comforting.

"Betty is crying in her room." Well, at least she was safe. "And Nancy is still out. However, I've phoned Juneau's room persistently every quarter hour for the past hour and there has been no response. You know Nancy is prey to mosquitoes, so no scandalous activity is likely to occur outdoors, or anywhere for that matter. Nancy is a good girl and Betty at least tries. The phone call was merely precaution. What's more, I've examined the Juneau clippings over and over again and I can't imagine what you saw in them to cause anxiety. Now, I'm very tired dear, jet lag or whatever, possibly old age, too, and I'm going to bed."

"Don't you talk old age to me," scolded Suzanne. "You're only 52, but I'll be up soon."

The music had all but ended. Sounds of "Good Night Sweetheart" emanated from the orchestra in the distance, and a peek inside the ballroom revealed a straggle of dancers remaining. The night club was dark and the lobby had a scattering of couples en route to rooms. Downstairs the cocktail lounge was empty, and the coffee shop had posted its closing sign, although a handful of people lingered still. All this Suzanne quickly ascertained. Nancy was probably on the way to their suite at this moment. Racket in hand, Suzanne waited for the elevator. The gnawing disease would not go away. Impulse caused her to press the button for the floor below her own. She had gotten off at the wrong floor, was tired, mistaken her room, drunk a bit too much—excuses, like champagne, flowed through her head, for listening at someone's door would be otherwise viewed as either gall or madness. The men they had vacationed here to meet had booked adjacent rooms. They were grouped at the end of the hall, in the vicinity of the Margot suite above.

"Let their doors remain shut," she prayed, and after 2 o'clock in the morning there was no reason that they should not. Her tennis shoes padded noiselessly to their destination. Suzanne glanced behind her. The corridor was still empty. She put her ear to Juneau's door, insisting she would hear nothing and would silence her doubts about the man. She shot upright. "Floor boards," she told herself. "The floors are carpeted," she muttered. "And they don't talk." Surely she had just missed Nancy and Juneau in the lobby; surely Nancy was half asleep in her own bed at this very moment; surely Juneau was preparing for likewise in his room. She longed to dial his room to make sure! In the middle of the hall hung the floor phone. She requested a connection to his room. It was with difficulty that she kept herself from tapping her toe with impatience as the room phone rang and rang, and with something akin to fright that she replaced the receiver in its cradle. The thing to do was to go to bed and not to go snooping; that's all a return to Juneau's door would be. And the door was shut, thank goodness, so even a snoop would gain nothing from a revisit. The beautiful brunette on the plane entered her thoughts. Still. Still, it was none of her business if Nancy was all right. She pressed the button for the elevator.

Suzanne lit the table lamp in the foyer of their suite. She then proceeded to look in on her sisters. Betty lay rolled up like a ball, emitting whistling noises. Like those she so enjoys receiving, thought Suzanne. She made a quiet exit. Nancy, having spotted the light under her door, sat up in bed, waiting with glowing face for her sister's entrance. Suzanne gave her a big hug.

"It went well, I see."

"Zanny, he's a darling man, so complex, so interesting."

"Are you sure there's more to him than an accent and a pose?"

"Oh, yes! Why he knows everything about everything! He reads tons of books and magazines about politics and science and food and wine and sports. He has a fantastic knowledge of history. He held me spellbound, and I always thought history and politics boring!"

"Did you have a chance to say anything at all?"

"Zanny, that's unfair. Of course I did. Philippe is a true gentleman, not a pompous, pleasure-seeking Casanova like Harry Bellemore. Betty poured her heart out to Mama, but she wouldn't give me the satisfaction, as if I wanted her to be miserable; I want her married as much as you and Mama do. But Philippe is a real man, with character and respect for a lady. Frankly, it was almost insulting, until I reminded myself about Harry Bellemore. Not a pass or an off-color joke. He treated me like another person!"

"I'm sure he was acting very—controlled."

"I don't think so. He laughed, joked, and told stories; he seemed very relaxed."

"And what else did you talk about?"

"Oh, work, and Mama, and Betty—well it seemed like the most natural thing in the world. He's so easy to talk to, and he was very sympathetic. I told him about all the wonderful places I keep reading about and how I'd love to visit them some day. He said he'd revisit them all with the right woman, if she were his wife. He gave me a meaningful look when he said that. He's all for marriage, 100%."

"Apparently he liked it enough his first three tries."

"Zanny! He's one of Mama's Big Four. Don't you want me to be happy? You're much more suitable for George, and he needs you."

Suzanne reddened. "Of course I want you to be happy, and I'm not interested in either Philippe or George for myself. I only want you to be sure the first time and not have to suffer through three trials before the match is right. I spoke of you to Derek tonight, and he seemed interested. I don't think he knows much about history or science, but he's a musician, an artist, and delightful company. You shouldn't narrow the field before examining it thoroughly. You've got an abundance of riches. Enjoy them; there's no rush."

"Mama thinks differently. Still, if Mr. Derek Barnesforth wants to charm me, I'll let him, but Philippe comes first. A bird in the bush sort of thing. I'll try to avoid Charles. He follows me everywhere. He looked so unhappy when he saw me with Philippe that I felt guilty. I don't know why; I don't owe him anything. He's got his job and I've got mine. But it's awkward. He's such a sweet young man. I hate to hurt him."

Suzanne kissed Nancy good-night and hurried to her bed in eager anticipation of hugging the pillow and sinking into the mattress and sleep. Instead she stayed awake for what remained of the night, machinations of romance swimming through her brain, and she wound up anticipating the morning and the required action as she had the now forgotten rest.

So you see, darling, Mr. Crump is in a socially untenable position. He has denied his own mother and could not possibly brook the embarrassment of my introduction by you."

"Mother, I have no personal interest in George Crump."

"Therefore, I will have to assume some other identity for purposes of introduction, so that later, when you admit the awkwardness of vacationing with one's mother, he can freely do the same."

"Mother, listen to me. My interest in marrying George Crump is nil. If you're so anxious to make him family why don't you marry him yourself?"

"Don't be silly, dear. If Mr. Bellemore is more to your liking, I'm sure I won't stand in your way, but you say you get on well, and he should not be discarded prematurely. I doubt that Mr. Bellemore realizes he has acquired a new mother and he should be informed of this to spare Mr. Crump public embarrassment. I want you to undertake to do that right after breakfast. If Mr. Bellemore evinces no surprise then we'll know he has been told. Whatever private anger he vents at his friend is none of our business. Our business is to enchant as many of these four select men with my daughters as possible. Object: matrimony."

"This is a horrible way to get a husband; it's so degrading! I'm not sure I want to marry altogether!"

"I understand, dearest, but chance is fickle. I will never be sure your sisters are secure without wealth and comfort. The cushion of money can cover a multitude of distresses, should they arise. With Betty they are bound to arise; with Nancy, I don't know. She lacks insight. Money can buy that and mitigate the hurt when it fails to. But whether you are rich or poor, I will always have confidence in you, dear Suzanne, for you are secure within yourself. You don't need a cushion or a backup or a name, and that is why you deserve them all—and more. I don't want the best for you because you need it, but you must forgive a mother's wanting the moon and the stars for her precious other self."

Suzanne clasped her mother to her, and her watering eyes spoke. It was with renewed determination that she vowed to set about the business of the day.

Betty stumbled into the sitting room rubbing the sleep from her eyes. "Morning."

"Good morning, dear. Hurry into the shower; I want to talk to you awake. It's already 8 o'clock."

"Only 8 o'clock? This is my vacation, Mama!"

"A working vacation, and at the moment you are in no condition for work. Now hurry, dear." And she gently pushed her in the direction of the shower and turned to face her eldest. "So you will speak to Mr. Bellemore this morning and get Nancy and Mr. Barnesforth together. His initiative may have vanished with the night. This afternoon you will introduce me to Mr. Crump as somebody or other, and I will effect a meeting with his mother before the day is gone. You will leave yourself open to the attentions of Messrs. Bellemore and Crump. Nancy will do likewise with Messrs. Barnesforth and Juneau. I will stay with Betty. Possibly Mr. Bellemore's interest may revive, possibly some wealthy unknown at the hotel will seek her out. We must be realistic and expend effort where it seems most likely to produce results. This vacation, Betty seems least likely."

Suzanne nodded grimly, but her determination to prove otherwise escalated. This vacation, oh yes. This vacation, and there would be other vacations, vacations on top of vacations until Betty wore triple strength bifocals and walked with a cane. Oh no! This vacation would be *the* vacation. The doorbell rang.

"Open the door, dear. It must be breakfast."

Suzanne opened the door to the mustached waiter of the day before. "Thank you, Pedro. How is your wife?"

Pedro stared into her questioning, gray eyes. There were dark circles under them. He wanted to kiss them away. "Is doing fine. Soon I be a father; not yet, but soon, soon," he said, addressing her lips, which were not full, but which paired irresistibly with her Grecian nose.

"You have breakfast for us?" Suzanne suggested.

"Yes, of course, the breakfast." And he wheeled the laden cart into the sitting room. He was relieved at Betty's absence and moved at the quiet gathering of three good-looking women for the morning meal. Nancy, her face placid, stretched and stifled a yawn with her hand as she gazed out into the shrubbery and trees. The older woman smiled pleasantly at him, thanked him, and tipped him well. Her features were, taken individually, delicate, taken together, a picture of charm and grace. Her voice, authoritative but kind, rang through the suite.

"Betty, you mustn't drown, dear; your breakfast will get cold."

Altogether a lovely family portrait of a male-less family, an appealing portrait, he could not deny it. He had not come there to deny it. He could see himself in it quite well. His eyes met Suzanne's. They had been watching him and he felt awkward. He pocketed his tip and quickly bowed himself to the door. His sweaty palms had no success with the knob, and he felt Suzanne's hand on top of his turning it. He turned in the corridor and looked at her again.

"My wife like you, señorita—very sad, very beautiful."

And the waiter was gone, leaving her with the apprehension that this was the beginning of a strange day.

"As soon as you and Nancy have breakfast, I think you should be off on your affairs."

"I'm afraid we may not see much of the men today, Mother. Mr. Barnesforth implied a full day of business."

"Well, if we can't seek them out, they will have to seek us out. Have they rented a conference room, do you think?"

"That would call attention to themselves. They're probably meeting in one of their rooms, Mr. Crump's again, possibly."

"Hmmm, 9 o'clock. They have surely started." She lifted the receiver from its cradle. "You will have to check, dear, since you would recognize their voices."

Suzanne paused. "Southern drawl," she decided, and dialed.

Mr. Cranshaw did not occupy that room; she had the wrong number, George Crump had replied.

Proposed Western twangs and Bostonese remained unused; Messrs. Bellemore and Barnesforth did not respond. "They're meeting in Mr. Crump's room, Mother."

"Then he's leading the conference—good. I like a leader," she said with emphasis, eying her daughter forthrightly. "Where is his room?"

"Directly below ours."

"Splendid. Perhaps a bit of stomping will bring him to us."

"He'll only phone, Mother."

"Ah, then you've paced already. Well, this time it will be of consequence. We'll wait a bit until they get properly involved. That should raise sufficient ire to warrant a personal visit from Mr. Crump."

"But what if he phones again?"

"We won't answer."

"What if he sends someone else?"

"Mr. Crump will see to the matter himself. It is his room and, I expect, his conference. The others will probably welcome the interruption, but he is a born businessman. That is the one area in which he truly excels. Mr. Juneau works at it, Mr. Barnesforth plays at it, and Mr. Bellemore cleverly concocts at it. Of them all, only Mr. Crump has an innate sense of business and pleasure in his career. Pace vigorously darling and his visit is assured."

George Crump grimaced. "I can't continue with that thunder overhead. She may go on forever out of pure malice."

"A bit hard on the lady, aren't you George?"

"Not at all, Derek. You should have heard him yesterday. We can move the meeting to my room."

"Absolutely not. She's got to learn that sensible people will not tolerate either noise or harassment."

"You're a businessman, not a teacher, George. It won't take long to gather all our papers, put them in our briefcases, close the tables, cork the bottles, and carry the whole shebang to my room."

"I will not be undone by a pair of feet."

Harry Bellemore lifted the receiver of the phone and held it out to his friend. "Those feet may be crowned by claws. Educate her the safe way."

George waved the receiver away and headed for the door. "Five minutes now will provide us with five hours of uninterrupted work."

"Make it three minutes," suggested Derek. "I'll be ready for a stroll around the grounds in three hours."

"Shall we go with you?"

"Thank you for your confidence, Harry."

"I don't want you hurt."

In answer George banged the door shut behind him. He had often been irritated with his friend without losing affection for him, but he was coming close to doing that now. No woman could be allowed to ostentatiously and publicly make a fool of George Crump, and no friend would want her to. He considered the stairs, but judged that the elevator wait would give him time to compose his thoughts and words. If a husband were present he would speak of business, of a livelihood, if necessary of bankruptcy. If the woman were alone he would speak of personal tragedy, of a life or death vacation, if necessary of a deteriorating wife. No lie could be too big. That pacing had to stop. He straightened his tie, adjusted his jacket, and knocked on the door.

The door opened a third. "Yes, what is it?"

George Crump blinked. The face was lovely, the voice soft.

"I am your neighbor from downstairs, and I want a favor from you?"

"What is it you want?"

"Some peace and quiet. It is impossible to work, sleep, or do anything of value with the constant pacing back and forth in this room."

"You've complained before, of course."

"You know I have, and I must apologize for the tone of voice I used at that time. I did not realize you were a lady."

"That's most generous of you. I'm afraid I've shed one habit for another. Sister Suzanne is quite aghast, I'm sure, at the behavior of her superior mother." She opened the door wider and turned back into the room. "Am I correct, my dear."

George Crump entered the room, his mouth ajar.

"Mr. Crump and I have met, Mother, and he has been forgiving of my error of the recent past. The pacing is more my fault than yours. It will not continue, Mr. Crump."

He sat down heavily. "You are a Sister?" Suzanne nodded. "And you are a Mother?" Eleanor nodded. "But why?" he asked, bewildered.

"Some choices are not ours to make, Mr. Crump," responded Eleanor Margot.

He looked from one to the other, uncertain whom to address. "What are you doing here?"

Suzanne, her hands demurely in her lap, allowed her mother to answer. "I'm here to see how Suzanne is getting on with her sisters. She is concerned about their welfare, their progress in this too mortal life, and I have given her leave to attend to them for a short while this summer. Ordinarily I do not leave home."

George pictured home—cathedral ceilings, Gothic windows, white curtains. He swallowed. "Is your home nearby?"

"No, Mr. Crump, it is not, and were it not for a frightening phone call I would not have made the wearisome journey here. I believe you witnessed Betty's indiscretion."

"She was robbed." He felt the need for a defense.

"One does not expose oneself to expose a thief, especially when the article of apparel in question is itself an article of exposure."

"Betty is young."

"It is gentlemanly of you to defend her. I believe another gentleman actually rescued her from the disgrace."

"That was Mr. Bellemore, Mother," provided Suzanne.

"Yes, another kindness by a protector, a knight. Men are much maligned, if you and Mr. Bellemore are representative of your sex."

"Thank you, uh, ma'am, but I'm afraid not."

"Ah, well, I wouldn't really know. I don't get out much, except when I can serve to bridge gaps, to serve as a bridge. The term bridge fascinates me. Sit down Mr. Crump and join us for some coffee. There are some tasty scones and biscuits, too." Her musical voice lulled him into acceptance against his will.

"Well, perhaps for a few minutes, thank you."

"Suzanne has praised your restraint highly."

"I must return it. She is certainly a Sister worthy the name. Have you been a Mother long?"

Eleanor Margot laughed. "It seems I've always been a mother. Endlessly and hopelessly a mother."

"Do I sense disenchantment?"

"I will not hide either the pleasure or the disenchantment. They vie for my commitment, but the pleasure always wins. Suzanne is a great help to me. Because of her, the house is always in order. Her devotion to others is exemplary, her unselfishness proverbial. She is a remarkable child."

"Have you ever tasted freedom?"

"Each morning in the garden when I inhale the first air of the day, before it gets polluted with economic woes detailed in *Business Week,* the hazards explained in *Today's Health* and graphically depicted in *Sports Illustrated,* and the mental cripples catered to in *Playboy.* Thank goodness for *Organic Gardening!*"

"Your knowledge amazes me!"

"Well it disgusts *me,* but I need it for my work. Suzanne is equally knowledgeable. We discuss all these important matters. But I haven't given her much opportunity to say anything. I'm sorry, dear."

George Crump paid no heed to her mumbled demur. He leaned across the table, and, unabashed, stared Eleanor Margot in the face. *"Playboy,* you say?"

"Men require a mother's help too. Of course, they don't usually realize it. One must seek them out and do what one can."

"How fascinating. What men do you seek and how do you help them?"

"You are too kind, showing such concern for my work, but Suzanne tells me you are a good-natured man of many interests." She gave her daughter a meaningful look.

"Yes, Mother; he adores gardening, as much as you do, I believe, and his organization and sense of propriety are at least a match for yours." For the first time within memory Eleanor Margot was taken aback, but her daughter would not stop. "Mother's devotion to others is so like your concern and caring for your employees. That orphanage Mother was telling me about, for instance."

His interest turned to animation. "It *was* a wonderful idea, much appreciated by the workers in Rioja. It was worth the Board fight to get it. You know about it?"

"Mother is always awestruck by genuine kindness when she reads of it in the world of business. So much is propaganda and pacification. Why, Mother was just speaking of your orphanage before you knocked. She was wondering whether it was organized along lines it would benefit our local orphanage to copy. Unfortunately, such details don't get into print."

A study in contrasts was the mortification of Mrs. Margot with the delight of Mr. Crump.

"It would be my great pleasure to discuss it with you over lunch."

"You are kindness itself, Mr. Crump, but I'm not free for lunch. However, Suzanne is free and would, I know, appreciate the information as much as I. We are as one, aren't we, dear?"

"I think it better if you received the information personally, Mother. I can take care of that other luncheon matter for you."

"Wonderful! I'll reserve a corner table in the dining room so we won't be disturbed. You shall have all the facts and figures you desire."

"But—"

"Flexibility, remember? Now, don't you worry. I'll see to the other matter. You never think of yourself, of your own interests. I must insist, Mr. Crump, that besides the orphanage you speak only of idle pleasures or worldly subjects and make no mention at all of business. Mother has enough of that all year, and I'm sure you do, too."

"I will gladly drop all mention of business."

"It seems, then, that I have nothing to say?"

"Not until lunch, Mother Eleanor."

"Eleanor is sufficient, isn't it Mother?"

"Mrs. Margot is sufficient," said that lady, whose agitated pacing was halted in mid-room by her daughter. "I would never have believed it of you, Suzanne. At least *try* a better acquaintance with the man, but if you can't bring yourself to do that, at least don't saddle your own mother with the task. Mothers-in-law are not so precious as to excite a man's extended interest. If you dislike him so greatly, say so, but to turn on your own mother, to sabotage her efforts on your behalf are beyond the pale!"

Suzanne embraced her mother. "Never, ever would I hurt my darling mother. When George Crump entered this room I realized how right he was for our family, and as the minutes flew, how right he was for you."

"Suzanne! Good heavens! Do you know what you are saying?"

"Very well. He is taken with you; there is no doubt of it. And as you would advise your daughters in similar circumstances, make the most of it!"

"I am 53 years old!"

"52, and what of it? Mr. Crump is not in diapers. He is as grown and mature as he is ever likely to get. He is shy, retiring, good-natured, and brilliant in business. You are ebullient, warm-hearted, sensible, and well-organized. You look beautiful; he looks sturdy. You have similarities and differences enough for an exciting marriage."

"This hunting expedition has apparently been too much for you. You've gone berserk! I am not about to marry a man years my junior and expressly designed for one of my girls. You have done a very foolish thing, and I am very annoyed with you for it."

Suzanne feigned a curtsy. "Ah, Mother Superior, the design was made above. I am the lowly instrument used to implement it."

Mrs. Margot took a playful swipe at her eldest. "What am I to do when my reliable daughter abandons control?"

"Do likewise—at lunch."

"I've had no thought of remarrying." She hesitated. "He's years younger," she insisted. "He simply won't do."

"Then you'd better hurry, Mother, because one hour with you and he'll be a schoolboy again."

"This discussion is unworthy of us both. But now that you mention it, this bit of nonsense may be of value. While I occupy Mr. Crump at lunch, the others will be free. You won't forget Derek and Nancy or to speak to Mr. Bellemore about his 'mother,' with Betty in tow, just in case?"

"I won't forget, Mother."

"If all goes well at lunch I may meet Mrs. Crump this afternoon, as planned, but if you're so determined to reject the son, there's no point to it. So things will not go well."

"Mother!"

"I will not waste the man's time, and there's the end to it."

Faithful to her promise, at noon Suzanne was at the elevator door when it opened in the lobby. She cordially but quickly greeted the eligible quartet, hastened off with Derek Barnesforth, and "accidentally" met Nancy idling near a counter. Mr. Barnesforth did not seem to mind. En route to scout for Mr. Bellemore and fulfillment of the second pledge made to her mother, she was hailed by Charles behind the reservation desk. She bit her lip in preparation and vowed not to lie directly. Nancy's whereabouts at this very moment were unknown to her, she rationalized, and so she told Charles, reasoning that Derek could have whisked her away from the hotel interior. Would Suzanne tell her to drop by his desk when she could? Yes, Suzanne would do that. Nancy's disregard of the request would be message enough for young Charles.

She found him swimming with sure, swift strokes across the pool. He surfaced at the edge.

"Good afternoon, Mr. Bellemore. May I speak with you?"

"Speak."

"I would appreciate your leaving the pool for our conversation."

"Appreciate? I doubt if you would. If you wish to speak to me you will have to do so on my ground—here." And he swam off.

Suzanne waited ten minutes for Harry Bellemore to revert to dry land, but he would not oblige her. She all but stamped her feet in impatience, desisting only because she knew he must be watching her. She walked to the water's edge, cleared her throat, and in a voice tightened by control and forced warmth called out, "Will you be long, Mr. Bellemore?"

"Perhaps an hour, maybe two. Put on you swimsuit and join me—unless you are afraid," and he lay on his back, closed his eyes, and floated across the pool.

The challenge was not lost on Suzanne. He knew it would not be. What a coil! she thought. She had no intention of donning a swimsuit for his delectation and without doing so he would not listen to her. She doubted he would listen well, anyway. He had ignored her in the night club, spoken distantly of Betty in the lobby and was done with the charade. She should be glad of that last, of all of it, in fact. Did she not admire honesty, despair of his trifling with Betty, detest the man? The blindly ardent Betty and the clever, mischevious Harry were no match. Could she truly wish him for her sister? When thrust into the realm of disorder, of whim, of passion, she could not be sure. There were no guideposts she could detect in matters of the heart. Betty wanted him and Betty's marriage was the pivotal one. Were she to marry and marry well, the difficulties of marrying off Nancy would lessen. The youngest Margot would rise to the challenge of the chase and the burden of Betty on Suzanne and her mother would vanish. At times Suzanne fell victim to fairy tales. She gazed around the pool. Most of the activity was taking place on the dining patio. The few swimmers and sunbathers were self-occupied, evincing no curiosity as she sought some means to extricate Harry Bellemore from the water. The means presented itself in the form of two little girls cutting out paper dolls next to their lounging mother. Suzanne spoke to them, and for the price of a shiny silver dollar received the loan of a pair of scissors. She would cut out paper dolls too. From his watery turf, Bellemore watched her warily as she walked to his lounge, appropriated his bathrobe and proceeded to do just that. He was at her side halfway through the first doll. He wrenched the scissors from her hand, threw her face down on the lounge and began administering a paddling. Her screams, muted by the lounge, brought no relief, but a lucky kick caught her assailant in the leg and sent him sprawling to the ground. Suzanne regained her feet quickly, but the agile Bellemore legs tripped her, throwing her into his arms. A struggle would have been to no avail even if the surprise and speed of events had been slower, for Harry Bellemore clasped her to him and covered her face with kisses. At last he weakened his hold and she was able to push him away.

"You are disgusting, repulsive, vile!" she said from the depths of her soul.

"Is that what you wanted to talk to me about?"

"You will make a despicable brother-in-law."

"I hoped I had made it plain thirty seconds ago as well as last night that I am intent on no such title."

"You are intent on it," she insisted. "It would be wise to make a formal proposal before the day is over."

"I will do no such thing."

"You may have forgotten your promises to Betty in the flush of your passion for her the other day, but I have not. I have a commentary of exactly what you said before you collided with me and Mr. Crump. Oral promises will stand up in court when supported by evidence. I have the evidence, both written and living."

"Are these ideas originals, Sister Suzanne, or an echo of perverted thinking by your Mother Superior? No, I didn't enlighten George when he astonished me with your holy background."

"They are exclusive and original with me, Mr. Bellemore. George is with my mother at this moment, as you should be with yours." Bellemore arched an eyebrow. "Haven't you heard Mr. Bellemore? George has given you his mother. You were night clubbing with your mother, entertaining your mother, showing devotion to your mother. It was most touching of you and convenient for George."

"And your nunhood, Sister?"

"A misunderstanding. Mother will speak of it to George."

"You have made a phenomenal mistake in crossing swords with me, Miss."

"We shall see, but I have justice on my side. You made a commitment and you must expect to keep it. We're a pleasant, easygoing family, actually; you will not regret joining it."

"Your viperous, vengeful, venomous family pleasant? Perhaps in some distant, distorted life. I will not join your family or any other, but prepare yourself for a countersuit that will put every Margot face on the front pages of every newspaper in the world. You had better pray you win this suit, for no man will get within shouting distance of any of you after this. As a minor aside, you have willfully, wantonly, and maliciously destroyed my private property." He threw the mangled robe over one arm. "George was wrong when he guessed the person pacing overhead was a whore. You are not that much a lady." And with slow, measured steps that belied the vein throbbing and threatening to leap from his forehead, he took the path back to the hotel.

"Wealthy men are never boring, Betty, and you *will* join us for lunch. I will not abandon you to the fancies of whatever men are floating loosely about this place."

"You don't trust me, Mama, admit it. But was it my fault that thief ran off with my dress and I was forced to follow her practically naked?"

"No one forced you to run after Alfonso in that condition," she reminded her daughter gently.

"The cause was good," retorted Betty stubbornly.

"I will not argue with you. If Mr. Crump is even remotely as dull as you say, you wouldn't abandon your mother to him, would you, darling?"

It was futile to respond, so in despair she dutifully followed her mother through the lobby.

"Betty!" Charles hailed her from behind the desk.

Betty rushed to him and with unusual warmth expressed delight at seeing him.

"Do you know where Nancy is?"

Betty looked salvation in the eye and knew she could not hurt Charles. "Oh, off somewhere. We can look for her together if you like. She shouldn't be roaming about the place for too long unescorted. I'm sure you appreciate the danger of wolves, Charles."

Mrs. Margot smiled, shook her head at her daughter and immediately understood Charles' quick agreement with her middle child.

"You haven't met my mother, Charles. Here she is."

Mrs. Margot did not restrain the laughter. "How do you do, Charles. If you feel my daughter has commandeered your presence for the next hour or so, you have my approval to resist."

"Oh, no, Mrs. Margot, I welcome it. I can see where your daughters get their goodness and their beauty."

"I will not thank you, Charles, since as a businessman you traffic in facts, not flattery." She laughed pleasantly again. "Good luck on your pilgrimage, children. I am off on my own."

Charles had an hour for lunch. He wanted both that and Nancy. They would have to hurry, he reflected. Charles took long quick steps, but Betty had no trouble keeping up with him. She had been a bona fide tomboy, and the daring of what her mother still called her adolescence testified to its former existence. Charles could move and think at the same time, and Betty was impressed. Questions poured from him as he crossed and crisscrossed the property. Had Nancy slept well? She had seemed overly tired at night's end. Had she gone straight to bed? What had she eaten for breakfast this morning? Had she remembered the tune she promised she would wake up humming? Did she usually keep her activites for the day secret from her family? Betty's answers were not as quick or as confident as the questions they addressed. He was worried and eligible, but he wasn't rich. Betty felt sorry for him.

From a distance they saw the couple walking along a treelined path holding hands. Charles veered off into the bushes with Betty.

"I gave her credit for more sense," he said, his face a rather bloodless mask. "He's a playboy with a long history of very unserious intentions towards women."

"Holding hands is nothing," said Betty, but the look on Charles' face protested that it was. "Are we going to hide here until they pass?"

In answer, Charles grasped her right hand in his and led her onto the path. He stopped before the couple and, boldly meeting Nancy's eyes, spoke in the most dignified tone he could muster. "We were looking for you. We thought you might care to lunch with company."

"That won't be necessary," said Derek Barnesforth. Nancy said nothing. Had she possessed the art to respond cunningly to veiled inferences, possessed the ability to parry surprise with surprise, Charles would at least have had the gratification of hearing her voice.

"The steak tartare diable is excellent," he pronounced, "Bon appetit." And nodding in the direction of Nancy's escort he walked off with Betty. He was horrified. He had been mistaken about Nancy. He had thought she revered the ordinary virtues of home and hearth as he did, but it seemed her home would have to be a castle and her hearth marble. He was sensitive to the obvious regard he had shown her the days before. He had been used, a filler, a mere plaything, and even less than that. He had definitely made a fool of himself and wished to be alone and eat ashes. Instead, feeling with her the bond of the luckless, he took Betty to lunch, where they had a satisfying exchange of woes.

Nancy's horror equaled Charles'. Emerging from a gathering of bushes, he had walked with Betty's hand in his. What nerve to offer the favor of his company for lunch, to turn with such speed from an adorer to an icy opportunist! And Betty, that poacher!

"Wasn't that the desk clerk?" asked Derek.

"Yes, only the desk clerk." And suddenly Nancy felt confused.

Eleanor Margot barely had time to scan the dining room for George Crump before he was at her side.

"Thank you for coming. We have a table overlooking the garden. May I take a Mother's hand?"

She smiled. "Perhaps not. I promise to follow you to the table." And as she followed him, she promised herself to disabuse him about her position in the world.

He pulled the chair out for her, and when he was sure she was properly seated he seated himself, rubbed his hands together and began. "Mother Eleanor—"

"You mustn't call me that, Mr. Crump. From your manner of addressing me, I'm afraid you have misjudged my position."

"I'm sorry if I've got the title wrong. I'd be honored to call you simply Eleanor."

"That would be fine, Mr. Crump, but—"

"George, call me George. The organization of our orphanage may be difficult to duplicate. We assign children to families who live on the orphanage grounds, so we help the poor as well as the parentless."

"That is most admirable and interesting Mr.—George—but not to the point."

"Ah, yes, forgive me. What would you like to order?"

"That is not what I meant. I meant that I have not come to lunch to discuss orphanages or even to eat, but to clear up a misconception. Suzanne is my daughter, my real flesh-and-blood daughter, as are Betty and Nancy. I must apologize for the seeming deception and ask you to excuse me." She rose.

Shock registered on George Crump's face, but as she pulled away from the table he jumped to his feet and touched her hand. "Sit down, please, I would like to talk about your daughters."

Mrs. Margot did not disguise her surprise. "Which one?"

"Why, all of them. I can imagine the cross they've been to you."

"Really, Mr. Crump! I have never thought of them as such. They're wonderful, exciting girls, each in her own way, and I wouldn't trade them for Croesus!"

"I understand that, and the name is George, but considering your situation they have surely been a moral cross, and I salute you for bearing it so well."

"A moral cross? What nonsense. All my girls are good girls and good children."

"I applaud you for defending them, but that was not quite my meaning."

Eleanor Margot stood up a second time. "Then speak clearly, Mr. George Crump. What exactly is your meaning? If you have not been casting aspersions on my children, pray tell me what it is you have been doing."

"I've been phrasing it badly, but what I mean to say is that you've coped alone too long with the problems children bring. I want to help you."

Eleanor Margot sat down. "Your kindness leaves me breathless."

"You are very beautiful that way," he murmured. "That is, your inner beauty and goodness are reflected on your face."

"Do not be deceived, George. I am a 52 year old woman whose goodness is most appreciated by the women to whom I have been 'good' enough to lose at bridge for the last month."

"Gambling is self-inflicted suffering, Eleanor, but raising three daughters is suffering enough. Pleasure," he added quickly, "but a kind of suffering, you must admit. The community knows?"

"About my losing streak, yes. Maybe that is what is undermining my confidence and continuing my ghastly performance at the table."

"I referred to your daughters."

"Of course. My good friends are more than sympathetic; they suffer with me."

Something in her tone displeased him, but he dismissed the thought. It was doubtless not pride, but a defensive arrogance that tinged her voice. He wondered how she had managed to survive the shame of two successive births and what kind of man could warrant such a sacrifice and indeed allow her to make it. And what had become of him? George's romantic notions, rusty from disuse, took fire.

"You are fortunate in your friends, then. I have a gentleman in mind—a brilliant businessman, but shy, retiring, awkward in social gatherings, as the nouveau riche often are. Betty might suit him well, help him unbend socially, cheer him, cater to him, and she would be amply rewarded in all the ways I hear are important to women."

Eleanor Margot unsuccessfully struggled to hide a smile. "Your knowledge cannot be all that limited, Mr.—George; you are being modest." He blushed. "But what sort of figure does this young man cut?"

"Continental, I should say, graying sideburns on a gentle face. Tall, slightly heavy. Continental and affluent."

"He's interested in socializing, then?"

"Somewhat, yes." He tried to gauge her thoughts.

"Betty is impetuous, you know."

George looked at her strangely. "You do want her to marry."

"It's every mother's wish to see her daughters married." And she whisked her thoughts away from Suzanne. "It may come to nothing, but we should try."

"That's very brave of you."

They both laughed.

"I love Betty. She's a lively, darling child. But disappointment has made me wary. Perhaps with your help I will be disappointed less often?"

"I hope not at all."

She pressed his hand. "You are being so kind, but why?"

He scrambled for a reason. "I have developed the greatest respect for Suzanne's efforts on her sister's behalf, a reflection, I realized this morning, of your own. Such concern for family is rapidly fading from our society."

"Suzanne *is* a wonderful sister and an exemplary child," she responded warmly. "I must compliment you on your taste, George, even if it seems to reflect favorably on me. You have witnessed her behavior, spoken to her, danced with her, no doubt."

"That last pleasure has not been mine."

"Then that shall be remedied this evening. Suzanne is a graceful dancer. One would hardly suspect what charm and talent lie beneath that calm exterior."

"I'm afraid my dancing is just a step removed from clumsiness."

"Just the kind of dancer she adores. She is no Ginger Rogers, you understand, but she looks delightful on the floor, and you will feel quite graceful and delightful yourself in her arms—as you dance, of course."

"I think I would feel more comfortable dancing with you."

She was amused. "You think me clumsy, then?"

"Oh no, no, not at all, I—"

"Well, I am. Not only will I step on your feet, I'll step on your hand and possibly even your nose, if you bend to retrieve the shoe you will have stepped out of as my heel squashed all five toes."

"I deserved that, but may I really hope you are as poor a dancer as I?"

"No, you may not."

They laughed again.

"You have learned a lot, considering your background, You're quite unusual."

"I am very much like every other mother, which hardly makes me unusual, and just what do you know of my background?"

"Not as much as I would like. For instance, your—that is, the father of your children—I know nothing about him."

Eleanor considered this. There was hope for Betty and Suzanne might yet be persuaded. Mr. Crump was entitled to some information.

"The father of my children was manager of the children's wear department of a store in Englewood, New Jersey. He was a good man, a hard-working man, an unambitious and generous man, and consequently a comparatively poor man. He died a dozen years ago, leaving little to support the girls and myself, but Suzanne had just entered the work world, and financially she carried the rest of us until Betty and Nancy began making their contributions. Suzanne is now a corporate lawyer, and Betty and Nancy are secretaries at a cosmetics firm. My girls are not lazy. They are workers, as your grandfather was, though I don't expect any will enter middle life owning oil refineries." Her words concluded on an up tone. But if she meant to suggest a marriage between her daughters and oil, George gave no sign of noticing.

"I am a worker, too," he said.

"And an admirable one at that. I was telling the girls so this morning." She made one final pitch for her eldest. "Suzanne said you and she spoke in unison for three-quarters of an hour!"

"But the conversation we are having is so much more provocative."

"Dear me, if you wish to be provoked, you must take Betty for yourself."

"Thank you, but my debonair friend would never forgive me for his lost opportunity. And I have a distant cousin recently graduated from Yale. I would be pleased to introduce him to Nancy."

"Your thoughtfulness really is overwhelming." I'm sure Nancy would be honored to meet him, in fact to meet any man of your suggestion. Of course, even with your generous and truly appreciated help, I must not forget that girls these days, even girls as wonderful as mine, are affected somewhat by a face, a head of hair, a superficial something-or-other. Female emotion and independence are fast becoming the hallmarks of this age, so I cannot guarantee they will properly appreciate your most kind and most welcome efforts on their behalf."

"Guarantee me your appreciation and I will be satisfied."

"That you certainly have."

He lifted his glass for a toast. "To you, the independent woman at her finest."

"Independent? Me? Practical and supportive, perhaps, but independent? I think you are misjudging me again."

"I think not, but a better acquaintance may determine which of us is right. Shall we say on the dance floor tonight before dinner and before I brave through the music with your graceful Suzanne?"

Eleanor Margot was thoroughly peeved. She had never heard such nonsense since—since she was sixteen!

When Betty faced Nancy across the bougainvillea her rage at the world had been somewhat assuaged. Male companionship, unexciting though it had been, had tempered her fury with the sex. Charles' agony etched in every line of his face and poured forth in a torrent of emotion had, temporarily at least, eclipsed her own. Charles had spoken for her and both shared and spared her considerable pain. He had enabled her to suffer some of the rejection vicariously, leaving her mind free to castigate, denigrate, and repudiate the worthless Harry. Nancy, however, felt neither relief nor heightened mental energy. Derek's charm had proven no match for her emotional temperature. His pastoral singing accompanied by an invisible flute had seemed ridiculous and unreal.

"Did you like Derek?" Betty asked without enthusiasm.

"Yes, I liked Derek," responded Nancy with unnecessary warmth.

Betty tore a flower free from the vine and mercilessly twisted the stem in her hand. "This place is boring. It attracts rich, boring men. Wasn't Derek childlike and boring?"

"He was not," Nancy replied hotly.

"I would have found him to be."

"Why, because the great hotel tycoon was so dull? You shouldn't judge the experiences of others by your own."

"You're very sensible for your years. In your place I would have thought Charles a wonderful catch before learning better."

"Don't play ancient oracle with me, Betty; you're only two years older than I am."

"For goodness sake, Nance, what are you upset about? You're just beginning to experience life. How will you react when you are my age and discover the depths to which men can sink to satisfy their sordid desires?"

"The depths to which *men* can sink?" Nancy laughed hysterically. "But thank you, sister dear, for the enlightenment."

"You don't mean to—oh, Nance, how could you! *I* wouldn't dream of stealing Charles. I'm your sister!"

"I've often wondered about that."

"If you're going to be nasty, I won't repeat a word of what Charles said. Think what you like." And she tossed the stem into the air and prepared to move on.

Nancy pulled her roughly by the arm. "Just a minute Miss Big-shot. You tell me what he said."

"I will not. It was a private discussion. I do not divulge privileged information."

"You were about to."

"You can't always have your way in this world, Nancy, and I'm sure that Mama and Zanny would agree that you are asking too much of me."

Nancy's beet-red face expressed her fury. Dragging her mother and sister to her defense was pure gall and pure Betty. "I don't care what he said, so you can keep your stupid secret. It's a pity you don't think more highly of him; the two of you would make a perfect match."

"That's what, Charles said. But I promised, so I'll say no more."

Nancy hurled her a look of the utmost contempt. "You trash," she growled.

Betty pushed her sister into the hedges. "You take that back," she barked.

"Embarrassed at the truth?"

Betty responded with her hand, and a moment later the two were kicking, screaming, and punching each other on the grass. They were pulled apart and separated by other hands, and a familiar voice overrode theirs.

"Stop this outrage this instant! Get to your feet."

The combatants raggedly chorused accusations at each other.

"I don't care who said what to whom. Such behavior is a disgusting disgrace. Fine wives you both will make! Fine daughters you are, too! Such demeaning actions put you beyond the hope or help of even this devoted mother, who has just sat through an insufferable lunch in your behalf." She looked at her disheveled girls—the scratch on Betty's arm, the bruise beginning to swell on Nancy's forehead—and reeled. "Oh, I can't bear it!"

Suzanne steadied her mother and angrily ordered her sisters to their rooms. The fury and the spite had left them, and they were frightened. They were at their mother's side now with fervent offers of assistance, but Eleanor Margot, revived in dismay, practically sprang at them with "Do as you are told!" She raised a woeful countenance to her eldest daughter. "I don't think I can survive another day here. Had we not been near, had someone else discovered them, possibly the men. Suzanne, the game is beyond my endurance. When the girls are thirty, perhaps, mature like you, kind, understanding, perhaps then." Her voice trailed off.

Suzanne hugged her mother, thought of her encounter with Harry Bellemore, and said nothing, Arm in arm they walked back to the hotel in silence, each step returning to Mrs. Margot her resilience, and superimposed on the picture of her bruised and bumptious daughters was the picture of George Crump and his desire to help. Her step quickened and her back straightened. She reflected that present hardship sometimes paved the way for future good. What good there was in damaged beauty she had yet to discover, as soon as she had determined its extent and remedied it as best she could.

"Hurry, darling; the girls will face the mirror and dissolve in tears. Nancy packed the medical kit, but heaven knows where."

Suzanne squeezed her mother's arm. Mrs. Margot was back in charge.

XIV

The mirror dealt kindly with Eleanor Margot, Surrounded by cosmetics, she seemed in little need of them. Her hair fell into natural waves, occasionally culminating in a curl, the mass of it brushed off her face and gathered behind the ears in no-nonsense fashion, in the manner of a bouquet, captured and contained. Her face was creamy smooth without the touch of powder awaiting use at her elbow, and the hint of peach was a rebuke to the pot of rouge she would shortly, though sparingly, use. Only the finest lines were visible near the eyes and, she reflected, she did not intend to get close enough to any man to make them cause for concern. For Eleanor Margot was proud, but not vain, not doting on the fine skin, the small nose, the luminous blue eyes. Even had the cares associated with a home and the marrying off of three daughters not been hers, she would not have made a celebration of her looks. But the pride she felt was real, like the pride of an accountant in a set of well-organized books open to public inspection. There was nothing of vanity in this, unless fulfillment of a youthful dream, the vicarious enjoyment of the successes of her three treasures, could be considered that. She hadn't fussed so with herself for years, and a slight thrill filled her as she recalled when she first had. Her mother had helped her apply the powder, and the rosy cheeks, and the black-encircled eyes. She had shut them in fear at a crucial moment, and the black had run down her face and stung her eyes. How she had cried and screamed! How her mother had rushed her to the sink for relief! She smiled at the recollection. And there was the first gala after her marriage. She had felt a presence behind her and turned from the mirror, one eye outlined in velvet black the other not yet done, to face the adoring look of her husband—silent, smiling, walking to her and kissing her on the undone eyelid, telling her how beautiful she was. The words rang through the years, the beauty of the words, not the face that had inspired them, and clear as conjured memory she saw her dearest darling still standing in the doorway leaning against the frame, his right hand on his hip. His favorite chair had gone, his clothes, his golf clubs, and even some of his books, in her thorough rooting out of self-pity and conscious pain. But the best of his presence had remained—its warmth, its love. She sighed and nodded at the mirror.

"Not bad for 52. You will serve your daughters well." And with characteristic self-effacing thoughts, tinged only slightly with expected womanly concerns, she applied the preparations on the table.

The door opened slightly and a head appeared at the side of the door frame. "Mama, are you busy? My zipper's stuck."

"No, darling, come in. Let me see." Mrs. Margot began removing the clump of strands from the zipper path. "This is a rather old dress, dear. I'm surprised you took it along."

"Zanny said it gives me a youthful, innocent look."

"At 22 that is hardly necessary." She pulled the last strand loose.

"Zanny says that looking fashionable is against my best interests."

"I quite disagree. You needn't go through fire and a thousand lashes because you were insufficiently clothed when you attempted to apprehend a thief. You look ridiculous; take that dress off immediately."

"Zanny will be terribly upset."

"I'll speak to your sister about it." Mrs. Margot suspiciously watched her daughter exit. Mischief was afoot; she was sure of it. She slipped into a robe and left her room.

Her eldest turned at her knock and voice and welcomed her entrance to the room. Suzanne sat at the dressing table much as she just had. She kissed her daughter lightly on the forehead and cast eyes on the dress carefully laid out on the bed.

"A lovely choice, dear. I'm glad you have finally decided to wear it."

"I wanted you to be pleased. I *am* trying, Mother."

Mrs. Margot lifted the dress and smiled. The neckline was provocative, the Empire waist was provocative, the plunging back was provocative. "And when I bought this for you *I* was trying, but our motives are different. You are trying to show me that you can try, but that it's useless and will I please leave you alone about it, and I am trying to get you to prove to yourself, darling, once past even provocative appearances, your desirability to the best of men."

The wry response was expected. "The others don't count?"

"Not for my daughters," came the stout reply. "Anyway, you have pleased me, and I imagine Messrs. Crump and Bellemore will be pleased too. And it's not as though you are starting from scratch."

"I rather wish I were." She avoided her mother's questioning eyes. "This is all so upsetting. I'm not sure whether I'm involved in a circus, an auction, or what. But whatever it is, I haven't the stomach for it."

"The courage you mean. You haven't the courage to see yourself as vulnerable to love, so you insist that no man could possibly love you and that there is no man you could possibly love."

"It's weakness to accept the status of an object, you know it is Mother, and that's as far as it can go with men accustomed to possessions—men of wealth, and stature, and hot air." In her exasperation a generous application of rouge had found its way to her cheeks. She slammed the rouge pot onto the table top and vigorously rubbed the red away. The rubbing had reddened her cheeks beyond the power of the rouge, and Mrs. Margot, silently acknowledging it, smoothed back some wisps of her daughter's hair and smiled down at her.

"You know my only wish is for your happiness. I'm willing to have you marry some pleasant man of your choosing—shall we say tall, 35, and poor?—without making a fuss. I'm sure there are many fine, decent men of that age who have accumulated very little in the way of material wealth."

"A man of 35 should at least be making a living. After working fifteen or twenty years, no man worthy of respect should be poor."

"Well," conceded Mrs. Margot, "making a living, then. You needn't marry someone poor. I won't object, darling, truly I won't. I do think wealth is preferable, but not to your happiness. Is there someone you've met here whom you're thinking of, or someone at home? Bill perhaps, such a fine young man. I've said so often, though I've never thought of him in terms of family. I'm willing to change that for your sake, dear."

"Oh, Mother, there's no one here but a nest of sex vultures and egotists, and you know how I feel about Bill. He's insecure, cowardly, and the dish rag of his department. If he were a real man he would get a job elsewhere with real responsibility that would make use of his enormous talents."

"But he would make more money, acquire possessions. He would certainly be less attractive then."

"You won't convince me, Mother."

"I know dear, but it won't be from want of trying. Actually, I came in to talk to you about Betty's dress. She said that you recommended that piece of juvenilia. Good heavens, I thought she had thrown it out long ago. Were you thinking that Mr. Bellemore would find more pleasure in robbing the cradle than in robbing the bank?"

"It is a bit silly-looking for a girl—woman—her age, but it's the only unrevealing dress she's still got for evening. I brought it here myself just for such an eventuality as we have now. Even Betty agrees it will be useful tonight."

"You're very wrong, Suzanne. My research has made me fairly expert on the subject of Harry Bellemore. You will find him trick-proof. He is a very clever man when it comes to playing at love; he will not be fooled. I've asked Betty to change into something more suitable. I intend to check on that suitability in a few minutes."

"Mr. Bellemore thinks he is clever, no one else being by to prove him otherwise. But I am a match for Mr. Bellemore, as he is finding out, and I am not playing."

"Oh, dearest, what have you done? Nothing dreadful or irreversible, I hope."

Suzanne bit her tongue—when had emotion loosened it so?—and sidestepped the question. "Betty and Bellemore enjoyed a mutual attraction. That attraction has not changed on Betty's part; it must not be allowed to change on Mr. Bellemore's. They are a perfect match. For Betty's sake I must do all I can to see it consummated properly. Mr. Bellemore will gain a pretty, vivacious wife, for which he should be grateful."

"Oh, my poor darling, they are a dreadful match! Betty is an immature child, meant for a simpler man, a man of ordinary sense who can steer her straight when her fancies override her judgment and who can financially and emotionally afford them. Mr. Bellemore does not require prettiness or vivacity; he requires a woman of sophistication, sense, and wit. It would be dreadful to inflict them on each other, even if we could.

"Mr. Bellemore's past choices hardly reflect the needs you have enumerated," she said dryly.

"Mr. Bellemore has not been in love before."

"I will not waste Mr. Bellemore," she said stubbornly.

"I certainly hope you will not; that is why I was so delighted he made part of the quartet."

"Mother, you're not starting that again; I will not have Mr. Bellemore and he will not have me."

"Have you two discussed it?" she asked roguishly.

"I—I'm sorry to say, for Betty's sake, that we are past discussion. A cool relationship has degenerated into a ditch. It had to get worse, Mother, I had to make it worse to jolt him into reality and out of his toyland. Betty is a real, live, throbbing female, and she must be taken into account as such. She is not a toy, and I have made it clear to Mr. Bellemore that I will not allow her to be treated as one."

"What have you done?" whispered Mrs. Margot, barely trusting herself to endure the answer.

"I will not tell you. There is nothing to worry about; I have everything well in hand. Please don't question me."

Eleanor Margot listened to the firmness of her daughter's tone with amazement. Even more than the voiced defiance it stunned her.

"You will tell me and this very instant!"

Suzanne moved energetically about the room to keep from shaking. She selected accessories with unusual panache and. determination. She said nothing; her voice would not have come in any case.

"Never did I expect to hear such arrogance from you. If I have raised you to this, to have neither respect nor confidence in your mother, then there is no hope I have done better by your sisters. I have wasted my life for you and am getting the thanks I deserve." She left the room in considerable agitation, slamming the door shut behind her.

In truth, Mrs. Margot had enjoyed her life, had reveled in the strategy sessions of romantic intrigue and the preparations for house parties and church socials that had peppered the years and spiced the bridge meetings with friends similarly engaged.

But she had never been an outsider, and her favorite daughter's silence on the matter closest to her heart had made her one. Even if Suzanne had done some horrendous, unthinkable thing, a mother, *this* mother should be told. Distraught, she twisted on the sofa, the obvious model for her pacing offspring. The thought of such rejection was more than she could bear and, as was usually the case when her limits of endurance were tested, she rationalized an exit from it. Exclusion was miles from Suzanne's mind. She wished to spare her mother worry and unpleasantness as she had said. Suzanne never lied. She was reliable. Her judgment lacked the cachet of the years, but her sense could not be doubted. She was sparing her mother the pain of sharing in a daring enterprise—and sparing her the pleasure, too. Mr. Margot felt better, dissatisfied, but better, and was, she believed, enough herself to pass judgment on Betty's choice of dress. From her middle child she might yet gain enlightenment about Suzanne's scheme.

In that she was wrong, for Suzanne had divulged her plans to no one. In her room she trembled. Only pacing relieved the tension, and she took no thought at all to the effect this would have on the occupant of the room below. She adored her mother and the pain of hurting her was real. But the truth would forever topple her from her mother's esteem, and she could not face that. Her mother was not prone to faint, but how else would a woman react to the statement that the daughter she respected most had threatened to sue a clever, wealthy man as stubborn as she in order to persuade him to marry her flighty sister. The stupidity of this course of action was insupportable and could, as Harry Bellemore had pointed out, redound to the shame and blacklisting of said sister and the Margot clan from the society it, with the exception of Suzanne herself, aspired to enter. But her tenacity to continue along this line had not diminished. Insane though it seemed on the surface, she was sure that a fiery offensive was necessary to pierce a stolid defense. She would not implicate her mother lest, unthinkable though the thought, the enterprise should fail. Neither would she have Betty share the blame if she were unsuccessful. She cared not a whit about the effects of failure on herself as long as she could shield her family from it, and she felt certain she could. The success or failure would be hers, hers alone, and she could almost taste the joy of success against her arrogant, unyielding, unappreciative adversary. Harry Bellemore would be punished. The Margot will would prevail. She had threatened Bellemore and told Betty to avoid him for the night. The preliminaries had been attended to. A drastic fall from grace required a drastic rise, and she was determined that Betty would rise, rapidly and well! She would sacrifice herself for that gladly, for out of the ashes of sacrifice would rise a free woman. She regretted her mother's arrival; the events of this night would pain her, but she had given her a taste of pain this night already. The sooner the escapade commenced, the sooner it would end and allow her to draw the curtain of sleep against the outrageous indignities and machinations of the hunt.

XV

A mere scattering of people brushed the lobby. Suzanne looked efficiently around. A few couples listlessly talked or idly wandered seeking something to do. Several "runners" were exercising their eyeballs on a group of young women huddled together for the usual counsel and safety. Suzanne shot the men a message of her own before discarding them. Her men were not to be seen, which was not surprising. They were not mining a territory; even the opprobrious Harry Bellemore was above that. The ballroom was her destination—and the library, the cocktail lounge and the coffee shop. She had fairly well decided where it would be, but thoroughness was never a mistake and she was, whenever possible, thorough. When she had completed her rounds she took a walk in the garden. She needed the cool night air to free her senses for a calculated perpetration of the night's events. It was steel for the mind. It stiffened her resolve. She moved briskly. The lights that lined the meandering path and warmed it did not warm Suzanne. They merely helped her see where she was going. No romantic symbolism for her. This was her night, not nature's. Despite its seeming aimlessness, the path led in a circular fashion back to the hotel, as Suzanne had found out after her embarrassing entrapment there in pursuit of Betty. Her mind, fittingly chilled by the air and occupied with thoughts of things to come, did not apprehend an encounter, and so when it occurred, when she collided forcefully with a figure coming in the opposite direction it was a shock, and Suzanne was in no mood to be shocked. She pulled back, and when the light shining straight down upon the figure revealed it to be Harry Bellemore she was very angry.

"You clumsy fool!"

"I beg your pardon." The voice was cold, correct.

Suzanne brushed by him and hurried on. Seconds later she heard him behind her. She turned on him. "You were headed away from me. There is no need to alter your course." She gave him her back and was about to hasten away when she was spun around by firm, unyielding hands.

"I will not be spoken to that way."

"Leave and you will not be spoken to at all."

"You do not own the air and the trees, my fine lady."

"Never use the term 'my' when referring to me. If you will remove your hand from my shoulder, I will be pleased to resume my walk."

His hand loosened, but remained. "I cannot understand such hate."

His words infuriated her, and it was only with great effort that she was able to say in an acceptably controlled manner, "I do not hate you, Mr. Bellemore. I want you to be my brother-in-law, remember?"

"I think not. One does not bestow such hate on a prospective brother-in-law."

"On a reluctant prospective brother-in-law."

"Especially not on such a one."

"I do not entice with honeyed words, Mr. Bellemore. I have no truck with pretense."

"You have made that clear. Are your solicitors hiding in the bushes ready to serve me with a summons?"

"I will not destroy your vacation."

"Only my life."

This was not Harry Bellemore. This was sham. "You exaggerate, Mr. Bellemore. I would like to leave."

He lifted his hand from her shoulder. "You should call me Harry, as preparation for the future status you anticipate. I shall call you Suzanne."

"You will do no such thing!"

"You do not want me as family, then. You give me absolutely no reason to believe you do. You tempt me with vituperation, disdain, ostracism, and threats. If pretense is anathema to you, if I am anathema to you, then I don't understand why you go to such lengths to dun me into keeping a promise made in the passion of a moment. Despite your version of honesty, I can only believe that your purpose is not to call me brother, but to torture me. I don't know what I have ever said to you to deserve such treatment."

"What is a passion of a moment to you, Mr. Bellemore, is something of considerably longer, may I say lifelong, duration to another, and the pain you inflict on my sister you inflict on me."

He considered that for a moment. "If I bring happiness to your sister, you will be happy?"

"Of course."

"I do not love her."

"That is of no consequence; she loves you."

"Aren't you concerned that I'll be an abominable husband?"

"Yes, but—"

"But that is of no consequence."

"I beg your pardon; it most certainly is. But Betty's charm and vivaciousness will remedy that."

"You think I do not know my own mind."

"I think that."

"I think, with all due respect to your honesty, that you do not know yours."

"I very much know what I want, Mr. Bellemore—my sister's happiness, and I believe it will also be yours, if you would only stop resisting. Apart from wealth, there is nothing more you could want in a woman, and I don't believe you would marry merely for that. And marry you will some day; you will yield to an inclination toward tradition. Why not now, with a woman young, exciting, and available?"

"Your argument would be more persuasive if you called me Harry. I would like to feel wanted by someone who understands me better than I do myself. I am not being facetious; I want you to want me. I will make no further promises concerning Betty—I've made too many already—but I'm willing to consider the matter and discuss it with you further if you can think kindly of me in some way, however small. You apparently believe there is some good in me."

Suzanne was wary, suspicious, but taken aback. "I can do that," she said evenly.

"Then may I complete this walk with you? You should not be making it alone at night." And he offered her his arm.

She hesitated, astonished, before taking his arm and passing under the bougainvillea with him, stricken forcibly with the unreality of it all. The proximity of their persons bore no visible evidence other than that; they walked with outward stiffness down and around the circular path. Within Suzanne astonishment mingled with vexation, confusion, and embarrassment, but her sense of humor was victor. The laughter began inwardly, but despite her best efforts it bubbled to the surface. Harry Bellemore, formal and silent until now, cast questioning eyes upon her. She averted his gaze.

"I'm sorry, but you must agree this looks foolish."

He stopped walking, his arm still in hers, and faced her solemnly.

"Considering our recent relationship—" The expression on his face caused her to discontinue.

"You find sudden changes cause for mirth. If they are sincere they are not humorous, and perhaps sudden only in detection."

"You must admit the change is radical," she said, wishing to repossess her arm.

"But it is real for you, Suzanne?" he asked, with the sound of a man willing it to be so.

She felt her breast heaving mightily beneath the shawl. It took all her wits to respond to the simple statement, and then only violently. She was obliged to tear herself away from her escort and step back. "You are implying distrust."

"I am praying aloud. Will you call me Harry?"

The vessels in her brain constricted she was sure, for she felt dizzy and weak. "For Betty's sake and for your happiness I will call you that, yes, Harry."

"Thank you!"

The weakness increased. His gratitude was intolerable! How she longed to run, from this spot, from this man to—to anywhere!

"You're not feeling well! You must sit down." His arms were about to encompass her shoulders, to lead her to the bench nearby stippled by the shadows of a tree.

The sight strengthened her resolve, cleared her brain enough for the utterance of a few disjointed phrases, and carried her away with the urgency unexpected of one hurrying to aid grown sisters prepare for the evening. As she ran she became increasingly angry with herself. Why had she felt suffocated, why was she running, why was her heart fluttering so? She reached the lobby with relief and shamelessly cast about for a place to hide; it was a necessity. She had to calm herself and return to the frame of mind in which she had left her room half an hour before. The lobby was awash with the colors of evening. The population had multiplied. The nooks and crannies no longer enjoyed isolation, and the chandeliers blazed overhead. Suzanne entered the bar. A dark corner would shield her from view and give her the place and time to compose herself.

Harry Bellemore's heart was in as chaotic a condition as Suzanne's, but his thoughts, though troubled, were clear. He was hopelessly in love with the she-wolf, the viper, and no quantity of regret about the quality of the family he wished to join could undo the emotion. Harry Bellemore, man of reason, business brain and careful playboy had succumbed to a woman. Not an ordinary woman, it was true, at least not the sweet-talking, ingratiating or calculating sort he conceived ordinary women to be, but a woman nonetheless. He sat on the bench Suzanne had refused to share with him. But she professed no interest in him, professed it with a vigor and boldness that would despair an ordinary man. Her vindictive pursuit of Betty's interests was admirable in a way, if it meant projection of her own feelings onto her sister. Admirable if it meant she was fighting to subjugate her desires for the benefit of another. Not so admirable if they were sincere, if Suzanne Margot cared not a whit for him and meant every word she had said. She had humiliated him by rejecting his proposal the night before, infuriated him by threatening legal action, come between him and his best friend, and reluctantly agreed to a truce if he would link his fate with Betty's. This torture she was putting him through could be nothing but calculation; she had to want him as had others before. Her outrageous behavior went beyond sisterly concern. All would be well if he waited, pliant, willing. He got up, irritated. The constant cawing of a crow had finally entered his ken. He strode moodily back to the hotel. Calculating—yes—devious, sincere, and calculating, but not as other women; no, never as other women.

It was with dismay that Suzanne saw Harry Bellemore enter the bar. It did not occur to her that she had driven him to it, but that it was most inconvenient to her state of mind. The frightening apparition of sincerity loomed large with the thought of him. It was unrealistic to believe that he could be in love with her, inconceivable to imagine that he would want her to be his wife, yet the signs were unmistakable. Worse yet, it was an uncomfortable feeling, not because the thought was inimical to her, but because it did not fill her with loathing. Yes, she could think of good things to say about Harry Bellemore; after the initial poor impression he had made on her when he had cavorted with Betty along the very path they had trod this night, she had found nothing reprehensible about him at all. No man of his stature or independence relished being pulled by the nose to the altar; this was a fact of life. Because it upset the plans she had for assuming an independence of her own was hardly reason for dislike. And sitting there in the darkness of the rapidly filling bar she realized that she did not dislike him, that she had shut her ears and her heart to him precisely because she did not dislike him, because she had meant him for Betty. Perhaps they would not make a good match; perhaps her mother was right. But she had chosen a path, a path of freedom for herself and marriage for her sisters, and she felt a duty to pursue it to its end. She and Harry Bellemore were not so different after all. What fireworks a match between them would produce! She watched him take a stool at the bar and slump forward over a drink. She took another sip of the bourbon she had been nursing and contemplated an exit without his notice. She was expected to be with her sisters, and she hated to be caught in a lie. She blushed at the realization that her effort to control the will of Harry Bellemore had caused her to lie shamelessly. She had prided herself on being above lies, but Harry Bellemore had made rubble of her pride, and in her effort to control him, she had lost control of herself. A good match indeed! A wretched match is what it would be! Her determination returned, and with it her wits. Suzanne Margot was not about to be bested by either Harry Bellemore or her heart.

Suzanne walked into the light of the lobby and the presence of her mother.

"Darling, where have you been? I hoped we would leave the suite together, as a family. After our spat I thought—you gave me a fright! You look gorgeous dearest, but you mustn't be seen drinking." And she removed the glass from her daughter's hand and placed it on the nearest table. "I'm sorry I was cross with you. I had no idea it would drive you to the bar, the liquid kind, that is."

"Now that's more like a sister of mine," said Betty approvingly.

Mrs. Margot turned on her middle child. "What do you mean? Have you taken to drinking without my knowledge? I'm speaking to you, Betty!"

"She was speaking figuratively," said Nancy.

"Figuratively? Betty never speaks figuratively. What do you mean by—"

This inquiry was interrupted by the advent of a man. So eager was his greeting that the discomfort of the moment passed unnoticed by him and was dispelled by his good spirits.

"Mrs. Margot, I telephoned your suite too late but prayed we'd meet before dinner. I've reserved a table for all of us. Please don't refuse; I've set my heart on it."

"We'd be delighted. We're strolling the lobby as we would a fashion show."

George Crump snatched at the obvious. "You all look so lovely." He beamed at them and there was an awkward pause. Mrs. Margot filled it.

"Such words coming from so fine an example of good taste are compliment indeed. Will you continue our stroll with us?"

George Crump beheld the handsome family and suffered a spasm of fear. Two scotch, straight, in his room had been insufficient to steel him for this encounter. The daughters came with the mother, and he doubted his ability to deal with the whole package. Without impressive concern for the daughters he would lose the mother. He felt decidedly out of his depth.

To the experienced eye of Mrs. Margot his uneasiness could not have been more evident. She wasted no time in dissolving it. There was his necktie to comment on, the slight wave of his hair, his solicitousness, and his gentlemanly manner.

"Oh, Mr. Crump, you embarrass us with your concern and your charm."

And George Crump felt equal to the occasion.

Suzanne begged to be excused and her mother could not detain her, but she watched uneasily as her eldest disappeared from view. Then, since worry with no foundation in fact was fruitless, she continued her thread of compliments in the basically one-way exchange with an appreciative George Crump, Betty and Nancy, bored but understanding, walking docilely behind.

When Suzanne appeared for dinner during soup it was with a drink in her hand. Her mother, eying the drink askance, urged bread and celery upon her.

"George's Rioja is infinitely better than this unpleasant-smelling concoction."

Betty, sick of the stultifying conversation and George Crump was impelled to comment. "You haven't tasted George's."

"It *sounds* better," reproved her mother. "All those sunny grapes and good soil…"

George Crump, flushed with something other than wine, nodded sagely. "Even Mother drinks it on occasion. She doesn't approve of liquor in general, except for Rothschild; she'll always have a Rothschild."

"Well, of course, George, they're so rich."

"He meant the wine, Mama," said Betty growing impatient.

"I'm sure she would have both," said George magnanimously.

Suzanne was surprised at the absence of George's male friends and said so. "You have abandoned your friends?"

"I prefer the company of you delightful women, as I'm sure they would if given the chance." He was all confidence.

"George, you are spolling us for anyone else!" exclaimed Mrs. Margot.

"I would like to do just that," he murmured in a low voice. "But there are two men who would he eager to meet Betty and Nancy."

"Which of the three would they be?" Suzanne could not stifle her curiosity.

"Of the three? Why none of them. I have two other men, substantial men, in mind."

"I'm sure he can find three, Zanny," said Betty consolingly, her interest in George Crump renewed.

Suzanne barely suppressed her mirth. "I'm sure he can find dozens."

"Yes, I can," their lone male quickly assured her.

"Thank you, but save them for those more worthy," said Suzanne.

George responded with fatherly admonition "You are very worthy. You underestimate yourself."

Nancy put her hand to her mouth. "I don't think so," she said.

The entree spared the seniors at the table further retort and repartee, and arriving glazed and flaming it provided a new topic of conversation.

Suzanne scanned the room for Harry Bellemore. She supposed she saw him in a far corner, his broad body leaning across the table toward a dark-haired woman. She winced. But it was not Harry Bellemore. The face that sent its glance about the room was, she could tell even at that distance, repellent. Not his face at all. She heard his name and gazed in its direction. It had come from the pale red lips of a tumble-haired blonde. But she ate with an ancient gentleman. Apparently there were other Harrys. Her scrutiny of the room was interrupted by the mention of his name from closer quarters.

"I have no idea where Harry is," said George Crump. "Probably deep in intellectual conversation with some gorgeous female."

"I would not mock my friends, George. I'm sure that Mr. Bellemore is capable of intellectual conversation with a woman, and 'gorgeous females' are not necessarily bereft of brains." The words flew from Suzanne's mouth before she could assess them.

"I was only joking," responded George Crump, still riding the crest of the wine and his success at the table to this point. "I wouldn't think of maligning Harry, though heaven knows he can't resist belittling me."

"What do you mean? How does he belittle you?"

George squirmed visibly, and Mrs. Margot gave her a warning glance, but Suzanne's eyes were fixed on George Crump.

"Well, he is amused by my dedication to work instead of the flightier affairs of life, my old-fashioned ideals, that sort of thing." He spoke as off-handedly as possible and attended to his food.

But Suzanne was not to be put off with this. "I believe Mr. Bellemore is dedicated to work; the success of his company would seem proof of that. And I believe he has more old-fashioned ideals than you give him credit for."

"Then whether in spite of or because of their similarities they make wonderful friends." A little laugh added just the right touch to Mrs. Margot's firmly worded statement, but she was not displeased. This defense of the absent man was totally out of character for Suzanne, unless she had entered a realm beyond her control.

"I'm sure Harry can defend himself admirably when the occasion arises," said Betty, "but since it hasn't…"

His name jarred Suzanne into silence. She had agreed to call him by his first name; to his face, at least, she would keep her word. She had not done it here, now. As if to exacerbate her, Betty asked with whom she had been amusing herself before condescending to join them for dinner.

"Not with Mr. Bellemore, I assure you." And indeed, those minutes in his presence had been anything but amusing. Mr. Bellemore he was and Mr. Bellemore he would continue to be. How dare Betty imply otherwise.

But Betty, not realizing she had implied anything of the sort, and satisfied that she had piqued her sister for defending her recalcitrant beloved, returned to her food with more attention than she had shown anyone that evening. Mrs. Margot recognized the sign and resolved to urge George to redoubled effort on behalf of her middle child, before that child lost her figure as well as her temper.

Nancy had smiled appreciatively at Suzanne's defense, nodded agreeably at Betty's retort, and generally kept her peace. With a ripening maturity she was thus able to avoid making Philippe Juneau a table topic, with the possible unveiling of her aspirations concerning him, dreams which would arouse opposition from Suzanne and envy from Betty. Despite her fondness for them both, she was beginning to perceive the pleasures of privacy.

Dinner proceeded without further event, Mrs. Margot and George Crump the only consistently active participants in conversation. But neither Harry Bellemore, Philippe Juneau, nor Derek Barnesforth, each of whom occupied various thoughts at the table, appeared in the dining room.

It was with considerable relief that the Margot daughters joined the lobby throng being swept into the ballroom by the music. Betty and Nancy cast condoling glances at their mother and nodded to each other their sympathetic recognition of her martyrdom as she continued talking to George Crump, surely the dullest man in existence. Suzanne understood the significance as her sisters did not, as she was sure her mother and Mr. Crump did not. It made her even more determined to realize the Bellemore-Betty connection. George Crump was to become family without undue obligation, cleanly, fairly, properly. Suzanne's first ballroom act was to order a martini.

"This is all so tiresome," pouted Betty. "I'd as soon, go to bed as stay up and be part of all this fuss. There are no men here, just a bunch of children." The elderly and married were, of course, of no account. Suzanne pressed the glass to her lips several times as Betty turned down dancing partners, fretted, and surveyed the room. "I don't see anyone we know!"

Suzanne responded with another sip and a reminder. "There'll be George Crump's cousin," she said as thickly as she could.

"But he's not here. Oh—there's Philippe Juneau with Nancy. I'd better go over and help her out. She looks positively flabbergasted by the man. Make this your last drink, Zanny, you don't sound so hot." And she made her way toward the couple across the room.

Suzanne put the drink aside and ordered another, a Rob Roy. She saw Derek Barnesforth dancing with a young woman who was little more than a child, and watched with approval as George Crump, during one of the saner melodies, led her mother onto the dance floor.

Harry Bellemore stood at the entrance to the ballroom. There were many beautiful women there who were the kind he preferred—married, one could tell—but he was unaware of them. His glance passed Betty playing aloof and Nancy in laughing communion with Philippe Juneau. It dwelt for a space more on George Crump, dancing seriously to a bubbly tune with Mrs. Margot. It finally found Suzanne, and there it rested. A rush of people at the door obliged him to determine his course, and he entered the ballroom. He wished to sit and observe her unobserved, but trying this he found he could not see over the many heads between them. He stood up again and, finding it insupportable to stand in the middle of a moving stream of people, he advanced to her side.

"A lovely couple," he began acidly, nodding in the direction of George and her mother. "You're next, I suppose."

"You have a singular manner of greeting, Mr. Bellemore," she said with some amusement.

"And you have a singularly inadequate memory."

Silence hung between them.

"They seem to be getting on well together—Harry," she uttered softly.

"So they are, Suzanne. Are you surprised? A couple with their ulterior motives should do no less."

"No, I am not surprised, and I make no sense whatever of your meaning." A touch of indignation crept into her voice.

"You make considerable sense of it. Remember your honesty. It is not to be paraded only when convenient."

"You do not know what you are saying," she said sharply, her anger stimulated by shame of the truths she had stretched so recently.

"Oh, but I do! You have turned my friend against me with the honesty for which your sex is well known, and with your clever tongue you have beguiled the man into a tendency toward you which he is cementing in his heavy-footed fashion with your most receptive mother."

"If you lose friends so easily, do not blame others for it, and this 'tendency' toward me as you call it, is nothing more than a fancy of your own."

"And you detest such a fancy, of course. You are above such a fancy yourself, preferring to imagine defects where they do not exist, and to twist sincerity into insincerity."

"I have never criticized your friend and I have never questioned his sincerity."

"I am speaking of myself."

"You are—you are mad!"

George and her mother were almost upon them, and it was just as well. So great was her astonishment that she could think of nothing else to say. She did not hear a word the arrivals spoke; Bellemore stood stony-faced and stiff. The import of his words came forcefully upon Suzanne, and for a moment she did not think she could breathe. She grasped the table behind her to keep the room from spinning, but George was prying her loose from it, taking her away from it by the hand, her mother all smiles and encouragement. And so Suzanne found herself on the dance floor, with George Crump stepping on her toes and bumping into her on turns, as she mechanically followed the rhythm in the distant portion of her mind. It was inconceivable, but there it was! Harry Bellemore was in love with her! It took three dances for the wonder to pass and for the struggle to regain her senses to meet with a modicum of success.

"You dance wonderfully well; your mother was right." George walked her off the dance floor, his hands in his pockets. "I hope it hasn't been too painful for you."

"George, you are the most cheerful dance partner I've had within recent memory, and that more than compensates for any lapse from form; you have not bruised my ego, and that is the important thing."

"Thank you. Your mother said as much and I appreciate it. Do you think it is wise. I don't mean to criticize. Your mother is a wonderful woman and deserves to have what makes her happy, but the needy can be served in other ways. To laugh, to dance, to sing, to enjoy the company of men once more—she should have the right to do these things for herself openly, without shame, without her daughters as excuse. Her Order must be a remarkable one to have borne the burden with her through the years, but then she is a remarkable woman." The amazement spreading over Suzanne's face only caused him to press on. "Surely she has other needs, and there are other satisfactions to be had. I feel she knows that. What I'm trying to say is do you think it is wise for her to continue as Mother Superior?"

Suzanne's face was now completely crimson.

"Forgive me; my audacity is inexcusable. My concern for your mother is enormous or I would never have spoken. If to anyone, I should be saying this to her. My cowardice is unpardonable. Forgive me; forget I spoke. Don't tell your mother."

By the end of his speech her embarrassment had turned to a desire to explode with laughter, which she contained by herculean effort. It was only halfway back to Mrs. Margot, who sat looking royal and benevolent as she engaged in earnest conversation with young Charles, that Suzanne felt composed enough to gently turn George toward her and address him.

"What you wish for mother she has; she need answer to no one for her behavior. There is no restriction, there is no shame, there is no Order. Mother believed you had this misconception, and she believed she had cleared it up. She is mother, wonderful mother, to three daughters. That is all. Having met us all, you must agree that that is enough!"

George looked in stunned awe at the generously curved Eleanor Margot, still voluble, still majestic and charming. "You mean she's always been in this condition?"

"No, George; she keeps getting better. And she respects you greatly."

He drew himself up to his full height, medium though it was. "If that young man is bothering her, I will not have it. She is too kind." And he approached the table, silently vowing to soon retrieve the mother he had foisted upon Harry.

Suzanne did not follow George to her mother's side. She was relieved Harry Bellemore had gone and dared not glance around the room for fear their eyes would meet. She was not reconciled to his love—she had done nothing to earn it—and attributed it to his love of the hunt, the challenge, rather than to any love of her. She was determined to pursue her plan for the evening. Nancy was dancing now with Philippe, so she would have to wait. A drink in hand would forward the enterprise while she waited. Dozens of others with none but the most obvious plans in mind clutched their drinks. Suzanne smiled at the irony. She was one of them, but her drink was no crutch. Suzanne Margot had never needed a crutch. She had been one all her life, she and her mother. This Manhattan was for the plants.

Nancy and Philippe were inseparable, and only a detour to the Powder Room gave Suzanne the opportunity to speak to her sister in relative privacy.

"He is everything Mama wants," gushed Nancy, before her sister could say a word. "Charming, attentive, intelligent, wealthy, and it's real, not like one of Betty's romantic farces. Philippe keeps talking about his loneliness, about the blessings of marriage."

"What does he say they are?"

"Really, Zanny!" But her sister's question, concocted in facetious spirit, did not play facetiously. "Security, dear Zanny, security!"

"Is that what he said?"

Nancy looked her earnest sister in the face. "Well, not exactly. He said companionship, affection, support. Just what Mama's been pushing. It's security—emotional to him, financial to me, and both to Mama! He's ideal! And he's a very nice man."

"Both ideal and nice." Suzanne absorbed that. "Do you love him?"

"I like him. Mama says—"

"I know what Mother says, but Mother married father. How much do you like him?"

Nancy stumbled for words. "A lot. That's a stupid question!" she said angrily. "You can't explain emotions or measure emotions."

"Try."

Her witty Zanny was all solemnity. The effect was powerful in proportion to its infrequency. "I like him enough to be in his company a lot, to dance with him, and talk to him. He's so attentive. His company is a pleasure, and I'm proud to be seen with him—

he dresses so elegantly and looks so distinguished. I love his accent. There is nothing about him that I don't like. What more can a girl ask for in a husband? I think he's going to propose, and I mean to accept. Mama will be pleased."

Suzanne did not respond.

"I would like you to be pleased too, Zanny. I love you and I want you to be happy for me."

Suzanne kissed her sister on the cheek. "I love you, too, and I want you to love the man you marry at least as much."

"That's impossible!" she cried. "You're my own dear sister."

"And Philippe Juneau is a stranger, a kind stranger, whom you merely like a lot."

"I've never lectured you about marrying, but I've been nice to George Crump on your account, because I thought you might consider an attachment. He's dull, boring, banal, and boorish despite his money, and he's a mama's boy to boot, but did I sound off about these things? Did you hear me say that spinsterhood would be better than George Crump? I kept my peace because I want you happy, and we are not alike; we have different needs. I didn't knock yours; why should you knock mine? Why dash my spirits with questions about a super catch like Philippe? He wants me and I want him. Must you approve of everything?"

"I would have appreciated your loving arguments against George Crump, though I would not have agreed with your conclusions about him. There is a sweetness in his nature, a boyish incompetence in unimportant matters. He will make an appealing addition to the family."

"You're marrying him?"

"No."

"Then what are you talking about?"

"I'm talking about misjudging people and following your head without sufficient reference to your heart."

"I've referred to my heart."

"And what did it have to say about Charles?"

Nancy was silent for a moment. "Charles has nothing to do with this."

"I beg to differ with you. Charles has everything to do with this. He's been besieging Mother for her help in winning you. He's always hanging about where you are. He was sneaking peeks at you from between the geraniums at the dining room entrance all through supper. He's been in the garden eying our window each evening we were dressing for dinner and the nonsense beyond. He's got a career, a goal, and he's in love with you."

"He thinks he's in love with me; he's young."

"And you think you're in love with Philippe Juneau, and you're young."

"I never said I was in love with Philippe. I said I liked him a lot. I'm being realistic, as you used to be. Whatever has gotten into you?"

The thoughts that crowded Suzanne's mind were not uttered: Realism is not in your nature, realism is for the mature, realism will not make you happy. The negation of reality was a negation of truth, a reversal of her long-held beliefs, and therefore fantasy and falseness. Why they swarmed through her mind she did not know; she had barely sipped the parade of drinks. Pragmatism and wit had always kept her world afloat. They had unaccountably and suddenly abandoned her. She drew the shawl close about her shoulders.

"Are you cold? Here, let's talk in the alcove. The air conditioning would be of more use in the ballroom; it's a steam bath."

"It's all that dancing you've done."

"You haven't danced enough!" she exclaimed. "You must dance with Philippe. He's such a good dancer. Please dance with Philippe, Zanny."

Nancy pulled her reluctant sister back into the ballroom where, regaining her composure somewhat, Suzanne allowed herself to to be led to Phillippe, awaiting Nancy's return. He seemed genuinely glad to dance with Suzanne, but she noted that the appearance of seeming unstudied and sincere was an acquired art. She was not averse to dancing, but had been too engrossed in observation of others and staring into an ostentatious display of drinks to assume that willing benevolence that indicated to the male that his advances would be welcome. She observed with some satisfaction that Harry Bellemore would read mischief into such dancing, fraught as it was with ulterior motives and conspiracy. She was pleased not to disappoint him. Philippe danced as well as Nancy had declared. Her sister's clearheadedness on some points held future promise. Such promise was not to be cut off before its bloom.

"Nancy mentions you often. Your influence on her is great, and I appreciate your part in the formation of her character."

"My influence has not yet reached alarming proportions."

"I think Monsieur Charles finds it quite alarming."

"But you are not alarmed?"

"Have I cause to be?"

"My new alignment where others have failed may sensibly be cause for alarm."

"A sensible alignment would not be. Experience often confers sense, but my sister has had no previous alignment experience. I do not wish to see her hurt."

"I am as you see me, as I have represented myself to be."

A man with a bad back, she thought. "Then you are an honest man," she said. She wondered with annoyance at this drift of her thoughts. Physique had never weighed heavily with her. It was that womanizer, that self-proclaimed Adonis Harry Bellemore who was twisting her thoughts so, she concluded crossly. But on reflection she realized that it was not. Harry Bellemore could not be blamed for everything. Philippe did not hold her close; indeed, he had not held Nancy close. He remained regal and stately throughout the dance. But despite dispensing with the image of Bellemore, she stirred herself not to compassion, but rather to an ambiguous fear. Phillipe smiled confidently at her and she was about to compliment him on his assurance when he assented to his right and Suzanne found herself in the arms of Harry Bellemore.

"You presume too much, Mr. Bellemore."

"I presume nothing, Suzanne. I enjoy dancing with women who detest me."

"You are a masochist; I will not gratify you." She attempted to pull away.

"George has given me leave to dance with you. Surely you will gratify George."

"What do you want with me, Mr. Bellemore? Are there not sufficient challenges for you elsewhere? Since you have rid Betty of your spurious attentions, you need not trouble yourself about our family. We shall get on well enough without you."

"Your presumptions are well beyond mine. Your arrogance and the liberties you take with my character find no match in any words I have directed to you."

"If you will unhand me you will not have to suffer them longer."

"Not until I understand you plainly. Are you in love with George?"

"How dare you question me so! Go ask your friend."

"So you can help yourself to another drink?"

"My habits are no business of yours. I am asking you to let go of me."

"I am making you my business. I will not see you hurt yourself or those close to me."

"I am not merchandise to be handled so, Mr. Bellemore. Nor am I one of your oil wells ready to gush at a by-your-leave. I am amazed that you persist in toying with me and my family in the face of these feelings. You are beneath any of us and your attentions, insults, and bullying are unwelcome. If there is a shred of the well-bred in you, you will unhand me."

"Your example has left my breeding in shreds, but I will gather what remains of it and embarrass you no further."

A retort was on her lips, expected—no—eagerly awaited, so she resisted, gave her back to surely the most odious man she had ever met, and fled in as self-possessed a manner as she could assume.

Bellemore's question remained unanswered. If he were so detestable to Suzanne, what did it matter? But he had to know. If her affections were not engaged elsewhere, there was hope. He was reduced to that. George had become mysterious, secretive. He had arranged a working dinner in town for the quartet and then failed to appear. He had phoned, mumbled something about his mother and hung up, providing lively conversation for the duration of the meal concerning the power of that eminent lady. George, ever slow to change his ways, had suddenly turned comet, even daringly stooping to use his mother to get his way much as she had formerly used him. No ordinary woman could have effected such a change, and contriving a dinner party with himself as sole male amidst the Margots, and his behavior during the course of this evening had made it clear that George had marked Suzanne Margot for his own and was not being shy in pursuing his objective. Desire had sharpened his friend's mind and forced him into boldness. Harry knew the futility of counseling a man in love. His own rigid belief in rational detachment from connubial bliss, in the sanctity of independence and bachelorhood had fallen before the demands of his heart, and he was no longer privy to his friend's thoughts. He wished George well; he insisted he did, but he would not be happy with Suzanne Margot. They were poles apart in temperament, in nature. Their marriage would be folly. Leticia would understand this, would agree. Her help was suddenly essential to him. If Leticia Candleby Crump failed him, George was lost to misery—and so was he.

Suzanne was an orderly person. She had planned this evening carefully and, emotional traumas notwithstanding, had been true to habit. She had set the stage for her performance, and now that the time had come for it she did not shrink from it. Juneau would be called from the room in a diversion, and her mother and Leticia Crump would be occupied for upwards of half an hour. She had been unable to determine a way to dispose of George, but the impending event would call forth all his manliness and sympathetic good nature. He would not be frightened away; his emotions were too strongly engaged. As for Harry Bellemore, that fickle explorer would either revive his affections for Betty or he would not. It was her duty to discover which. In her heart she doubted that he could be counted on and half hoped such would be the case. His unreliability was not conducive to a marriage that would settle Betty and provide happiness for her and tranquillity for her family. Nancy would marry Philippe, and the misgivings that match caused her would be balanced by the pleasure she would have in seeing her mother become Mrs. George Crump. And if tonight's final act of desperation did not snare Bellemore, it would satisfy Suzanne that she had made the ultimate social sacrifice for her sister—her public character, her good name. Her conscience would then allow her to bow to the connections and means of Crump and Juneau to assist Betty. She could live for herself from now on; this final sacrifice would entitle her to be her own woman, to find her own way, to live her own life, to be freed at last from the responsibility of being elder sister and the anguish that attended it. Her face flushed by relentlessly applied rouge minutes before, her lips parted in a smile to no one in particular, she placed her latest drink on the adjoining table and allowed herself to be led by a red-haired young man onto the dance floor.

Leticia Candleby Crump grumbled at the little boy trying to remain at the heels of his mother. Where were *her* grandchildren? Where was her only son, for that matter? She had been annoyed all day, annoyed, irritated, and bored. She had come to rest, to gamble, to see her son, and she had done little of any. Since Harry, with his eclectic taste in women, had threatened her into canceling the debt owed her by that brazen hussy, she had considered it prudent not to engage in her favorite recreation. Gambling was a mental stimulant. Did they want her senile? And George! What obligation did she have to a son who kept excusing himself from her presence for activities that pleased him more. She had every reason for anger. Ballrooms held no fascination for her without her family and old cronies. She was merely an old lady to everyone else, and being merely anything, especially that, did not suit her. Having dined alone in her room and played solitaire to distraction, she had dressed and ventured forth among strangers to find what amusement she could, even if only her son; her tongue was ready. So it was not with the tenderest feelings that she peered into the warm, crowded ballroom. Nor was it with anything resembling relish that she saw her son dancing with a woman. George could not dance; George had no business on the dance floor. Such foolishness would lead to no good. He would have to marry a Wentworth sister immediately; she and old Mrs. Wentworth had gotten on splendidly in high school. She would speak to Harry about it. Her satisfaction was short-lived, replaced by revulsion at the sight of Harry Bellemore engrossed in conversation with the elder sister of the hussy. She had often felt that men were fools, but seldom as strongly as now. She was forced to elbow her way to the bar for a glass of solace, and when she reached it these slights to her person and pride had made her ill-tempered. She called for Lafite Rothschild as for a cab, had she been accustomed to call for cabs. The negative response did not deter her. She energetically repeated the request, rebuffing the suggestions of the bartender and the surrounding clientele. A woman of distinction would drink nothing but Lafite Rothschild and Lafite Rothschild it must be, she boomed.

"Allow me to seat you at a table and I'll get it for you," came a voice at her back.

She whirled around to face Harry. "A fine watch you've been keeping on my son! Look at him! Entertaining low life, riffraff. Who is that woman?"

"Come, we'll talk about it." He led her to a table. "George is more his own man than we thought."

"The Wentworth sisters, Harry. I'd almost forgotten their existence. You've always liked—"

"Whom George should marry is a moot question until his affections have been disengaged from his current amor."

"I can't believe you've let it go this far. Why was I not told? Who is that woman?"

"Suzanne Margot, sister of—"

"Not the child, the woman!"

"Her mother, Eleanor Margot."

"My God, this is intolerable. I will not allow it. Look at him, simpering, drooling, being bent like a bamboo stick!"

"You would be wise to meet Mrs. Margot."

"Meet with the creator of that stripper, that siren, that hoyden? You jest! I will not demean myself by catering to trash. You may toy with them if you like, but a woman of my standing—"

"—must take care to preserve it. Better to spend a brief time in her company now than to have to live with it forever. You have had no recreation since our poolside chat?"

"You know I haven't. You must have alerted the entire staff, to judge by the watch I've been getting."

"You underestimate your carriage and the figure you strike. But I was mistaken; you deserve some pleasure."

"Ever gracious!" she snapped. "It is children who should be pleasing their elders, not the other way around. A pretty pass this world has come to! Well, I intend to right matters."

"And I intend to help you. Mrs. Margot is a bridge aficionado. Her luck has been bad lately."

"There's no challenge in defeating a loser."

"She's only been losing lately. Her luck may return. We should afford her that chance, shouldn't we?"

"Yes, yes, of course. Compassion demands it. A little table in the library, a few rubbers of Draw Bridge; yes, an excellent idea, Harry. And elementary politeness would suggest meeting an acquaintance of my son." Her face broke into wrinkles as her thin lips spread in a smile. She put her arm in his. "Let us not delay."

There was no hint of contempt in the greeting Leticia Crump awarded Eleanor Margot. It was of a mingled warmth and authority that had for half a century characterized her introductions to those she needed and despised.

"How good to meet a mother who accompanies her daughters. So many allow their young to live their own lives, and so few young people know how to do that well. A mother's guidance is so important. As much as I trust my George, I still like to make little recommendations when I believe they are needed."

Eleanor Margot smiled and inclined her head. No compliment, no rebuke.

"You arrived rather suddenly, I have heard," she pursued.

"To others it may have appeared sudden. Have you enjoyed the week here?"

The old woman eyed her shrewdly. "We are both recent arrivals," she said. "I understand we have another vice in common—bridge. If your boredom with this element equals mine, perhaps a game would be timely. Shall we say Draw Bridge? The library will do nicely."

George was crossing the floor to Eleanor, champagne bottle and glasses in hand. The sight of his mother made him visibly upset. "You've met?"

"Hello, Mother dear. How are you. I've been wondering all day whether you were alive or dead," mimicked his elder.

George blushed. "How are you, Mother? We've been very busy."

"*We* have? How exhausted *we* must have gotten, much in need of champagne."

"Join us for a glass, won't you?"

"A glass. Thank you, son," she said sarcastically. "You know I don't drink that poison. I wasn't aware that you did."

George unconsciously squared his shoulders. "May I get you something else?"

"No, George. You mustn't spoil me with so much kindness. Mrs. Margot and I are going off for a little game of bridge. We are leaving this nonsense to you young people. Try not to disgrace me in our absence."

Having properly aged Eleanor Margot and cribbed her son, she grabbed the other woman's arm and pulled her away, giving Eleanor Margot barely time to squeeze George's hand and point in the direction of Suzanne who was approaching them.

A lone male was in possession of the library. They appropriated a table to the side of the fireplace and lay their wraps on the high-backed chairs. Mrs. Crump removed a deck of cards from her handbag and placed them on the table.

"Shall we say five dollars a point?"

Mrs. Margot was taken a back. "I don't play for money."

"I do. It adds flavor to the game. I can't abide the dullness of playing merely for fun. I've had enough insipid entertainment in my life."

"Then I must decline to play with you." Eleanor Margot reached behind for her wrap.

"Nonsense. We shall play for something else, then."

"Lafite Rothschild, perhaps?" came the nimble rejoinder.

Leticia Crump's face fell into a thousand creases as she smiled. "Won from a woman it would ruin my taste for it forever."

"After which champagne would do nicely."

"I cannot be reduced by wit, Mrs. Margot," she said sternly.

"Have no fear; I cannot afford to have my finances reduced by Lafite Rothschild."

"You do not like me."

"I had no idea that you wished to be liked. I was under the impression that you preferred to be respected and feared. You have certainly won my respect."

Leticia Crump hit the flat of her hand on the table. "I shall play you for nothing," she cried. "You may deal."

She watched her unruffled opponent calmly shuffle the cards and with quiet precision deal them out.

"Widowed with three daughters—an unenviable position. Accept my sympathy."

"One spade," came the serene response.

"Double. You should remarry."

"Two clubs. Your example seems a wiser course."

"But you have children you wish to see married."

"What is your bid?"

"Two no-trump."

"My girls will meet their future husbands in the normal course of events."

Leticia Crump stared hard at her. "I take it you consider *this* to be the normal course of events?"

"Yes, I do. Much as we met people through business and social activities who became friends, brothers-in-law, or husbands, so should we expect young people to do."

"A luxurious out-of-the-way resort can hardly be considered the usual setting for social activities."

"The more out-of-the-way, the more usual it is. These days ordinary pleasures require extra-ordinary trappings. I doubt if you always bet at bridge."

"But I am old and bored. What excuse is there for the young?"

"They believe themselves old and equally bored. Pass."

"Trick." She penciled it in. "What do you think of my son?"

"I think he will be glad we are not gambling."

"I do not appreciate your manner of changing subjects," she said shortly.

"I was not aware that I had. You have a devoted son; that speaks very well for him."

"Devoted, yes, but I'm beginning to wonder to whom."

"Do you wish to continue playing?"

"Yes, I always complete what I start."

"Two diamonds."

"Two hearts."

"Your game."

"A social life is well and good in its place, but for my son at least this is not the place. He came here with some business colleagues. Female distractions are inimical to a man's resolution of business deals."

"This concern properly lies with your son."

"And his concerned parent. There is, I believe, some involvement on your part in this matter."

"You are mistaken. If your son chooses to dance with young women, my daughters included, I cannot think how I, or they, can be responsible for his neglect of work, if neglect there has been. I noticed his colleagues were also drawn into dancing and affability, possibly as a healthy counterbalance to the business affairs of the day."

"I cannot rationalize a serious problem away by calling forth the bogeyman of health, Mrs. Margot, and the behavior of other men is no business of mine. Your entire family is here en masse on the hunt for husbands. Your daughters' goals are not unnatural, their machinations, with which I have amused myself since my *arrival*, are to be expected. But a woman of your age should not display the same levity in the same pursuit, and certainly not with a man considerably her junior."

Mrs. Margot put her cards face down on the table and stood up. "You have just made an impertinent and inaccurate statement, Mrs. Crump. I am amazed that a woman of *your* age should speak so thoughtlessly."

"Do you deny you are attempting an attachment to my son?"

Eleanor Margot removed the wrap from the back of her chair. "I will assume the wine is the source of this derangement, and I have no response to make to the wine."

"Running off like this changes nothing. Sense should bid you to remain and address yourself to the matter."

"I entered this library with the expectation of a game of bridge. You are not interested in bridge, Mrs. Crump, but in innuendo and preposterous accusation. If I were attempting to throw myself at your son, who reached his majority some twenty-five years ago, I would hardly ask permission of his mother. I am all amazement! Good evening!"

"I know my son as you do not, and I wager if you turn your cards face up you will find I have a winning hand." She exhibited the royal family to her opponent. "The rubber is mine."

"And little else," said Eleanor Margot, and she promptly left the room.

It was in this agitated exit from the library that she encountered George Crump.

"What is it; what's happened?" he demanded.

"Nothing, nothing," came the almost breathless response. She inhaled deeply. "I've lost my ring, that is all. I must have dropped it in the ballroom. Please, you must excuse me!"

"Wait, I'll look with you. It's sure to be found. It *will* be found!" Visions of Cartier and Tiffany jewel trays dashed through his brain.

"You mustn't bother. Please go to Suzanne. Keep her from me. The child gets so distressed when I'm aflutter. She mustn't be upset—such a wonderful girl, such a remarkable daughter. Please, dear George, go to her. I'll be fine, and I'll find my ring."

But neither the words "child," "girl," nor "daughter," impressed themselves on George Crump. Only "dear George" resounded in his head and lodged in his heart. "I will not leave you. Describe the ring; I don't recall it."

"It was a knotted amethyst and pearl. I will find it with no trouble." George began a demur. "If you wish you may inquire of the waiters, but I am optimistic, really I am. You mustn't worry for me." She simulated a light laugh. "I must be more careful or soon I'll have a rash of young people worrying about me!"

Not the quickest digester of hints and implications, George was suddenly struck by her words. "My youth, if such it seems, is entirely of your doing. You make a man feel young and I shall not seek out Suzanne, who will see me for the middle-aged man I am. We will look for the ring together."

His tone brooked no refusal and gazing at him in astonishment she dared not offer one. They would search for the non-existent ring, doubtless the entire evening, in each other's company in shocking disregard of the proprieties regarding mothers-in-law to be. But George had dismissed Suzanne, forgotten his mother and her presence a few steps beyond the library door, and abandoned his male companions and all female company for the evening for her! The shock left her speechless and pale, and George took his hand in hers for reassurance. Leticia Crump's fears had been grounded in truth and would have to be dealt with immediately. George Crump with an interest in her? Heavens, this would not do! And Leticia Crump, watching their retreating figures from the library door, could not have agreed more.

A mother of thirty years experience is unlikely to be surprised at the exploits of her young, but nothing in the past had prepared Eleanor Margot for the sight that greeted her entrance to the ballroom. As moons orbit around Saturn, so were groups of people arranged around the lofty figure of her eldest, her feet dangling above a table for two, her hands gripping the brass mesh of wires from which sprouted one of the room's massive chandeliers. Melodramatics not being her forte, Mrs. Margot did not clutch her heart and faint gracefully at the feet of her escort. Instead, she pushed violently through the crowd to her precariously perched daughter and demanded she place her feet on the table and descend immediately. This order drew neither verbal nor visual response. Several gentlemen had mounted chairs and were attempting a rescue, but the danger of swinging heels made their efforts timid. Suddenly, orders were being barked by a tall, curly-haired figure, and the rescue party abandoned their chairs. Harry Bellemore jumped atop the tiny table with agility. He paid no mind to the table's sway his leap had instigated or the audible intake of breath from the viewers of his act. He soundly smacked the behind of the woman above him and was rewarded with the loosening of one hand on the brass wire. The kicking became more violent, however, and but for the steadying hands from those nearby, he and the table would have toppled to the floor. It was now Betty pushing her way to the fore, tugging at Harry Bellemore's legs, begging him to come down so that she could ascend and speak to her sister. Bellemore was reluctant, but the increased wildness of the hanging figure and his fear for her safety if such activity continued caused him to jump to the floor and lift Betty to the table top. Mrs. Margot was treated to such a display of compassion and urgency by the younger daughter that her shock at hearing it was equaled only by her fear for the life of her eldest. So it was that Suzanne was at last persuaded to touch feet to table and ultimately to floor. Betty recalled her sister's drinks, and in short order those who had seen nothing of them were recalling them too.

Suzanne shook off all proffered aid, including that of her mother, but she bit the inside of her cheek as she did so. Only Betty was allowed to accompany her from the ballroom amid most gratifying praise, gratifying to Suzanne, that is. Betty heard nothing of it, so intent was she in steering her sister to privacy. Her first words upon attaining the lobby were, "God, Zanny, I hope you didn't drop the letter!"

Eleanor Margot's movements were arrested by the fussing of George Crump, whose anxiety was the pale woman at his side. Nancy, however, was able to scoot into the elevator before the door closed on her two sisters.

"How could Zanny be so bird-witted," exclaimed Betty. "If I had wanted Harry to see all those nasty things I wrote about him, I would have sent him the letter. He spoke to me twice this evening. We didn't dance, but I think he was leading up to it. Zanny could have ruined everything if he had gotten hold of her and the letter. And getting drunk! What must he think of this family!"

"You're a fine one to talk," said Nancy.

"I wish you would both be quiet." Suzanne pressed the button for their floor.

"Zanny, you're all right?"

"You don't sound drunk."

"I have two perceptive sisters."

"What kind of gag is this?" demanded Betty.

"Shush!" The elevator door opened and the sisters peeked out. The corridor was empty.

"Is it a gag to make a sister the heroine of the evening?"

Betty's eyes opened wide as Suzanne ushered them both into the suite. "Let me have the letter now, Zanny."

"It's in the bottom drawer."

"*Was,* you mean, before you took it; Nancy told me. I should be furious with you for stealing it, for that's what it amounted to, but since your motive was good and since you've gone through so much bother for me, I can't be angry."

"How generous of you, Betty. But you know you would gladly have given Zanny a packet of letters if she could have used them to your advantage. Stealing! What would Zanny know of that? Rather your area, wouldn't you say?"

"And what does that mean?"

"I am quite capable of carrying on a conversation with Philippe Juneau without your assistance."

"I was only trying to be helpful. I told Zanny it seemed as if you needed help, didn't I Zanny?"

"You're never eager to help me with the laundry or the windows, but you fall all over yourself to help me with a man!"

"That's untrue. I—"

"Girls, please! I have a dreadful headache; don't argue, please— for me."

The sisters murmured their sympathy.

"Harry Bellemore must regret his inconstancy," said Suzanne. She hugged her younger sister. "If he ignores you now he is a fool. You were all loveliness tonight."

"You looked special yourself, Zanny. Whenever I glanced at Mr. Bellemore his eyes were on you," said Nancy.

"Shock at my décolleté, no doubt."

"More than that, I should say."

"Just what are you implying," said Betty curtly.

"That Harry Bellemore is more attracted to Zanny than to any other woman in this hotel."

"That's ridiculous! I will not allow such foolish talk. When will you two outgrow this senseless competition. You each have your own charms and will develop your own circle of men. I all but kicked Mr. Bellemore in the head and in the face, and I hardly think he found my manner then or in days past of any attraction to him."

"He came to your rescue," persisted Nancy stubbornly.

"And so did I," reminded Betty. "And if my motives weren't completely noble, there is no reason to believe Harry Bellemore's were either!"

Betty, having so accurately castigated herself, there was no further comment either of her sisters could make on the subject.

Suzanne stood wearily. "I'm satisfied. Bellemore was present when Betty rose to the occasion."

"You mean to the bait."

"I would have, anyway," protested Betty, "letter or no letter."

Suzanne rumpled her sister's hair.

"So you say. But Zanny had to put her reputation on the line, make a spectacle of herself before all those people before you did."

"I don't regret this evening. What people think of me isn't important. My family's happiness is. I scarcely thought of all that crowd once I'd begun. And we'll be leaving soon and are not likely to see any of them again. Bellemore's interest in Betty has been revived. That's the important thing. That pleases me."

"Then why don't you look pleased?" asked Nancy.

"Don't I? It's this beastly headache, I suppose, and I'm very tired. I'm going straight to bed." She kissed her sisters good night and went to her room.

"Fate is perverse," said Nancy ominously. "Who knows when or where she'll meet some of these strangers again. She's ruined her reputation forever—for you!"

"You all thought that I'd ruined mine after the beauty contest, but notice the comeback I've made."

Nancy's response was interrupted by the sound of a key in the lock. The door burst open and Mrs. Margot, a veritable scarlet, demanded the whereabouts of her eldest daughter.

"She's in her room, but she's gone to bed; she's very tired."

The door to Suzanne's room slammed shut on Nancy's final word, and in solemn silence the two listened to the fury and anguish of a distraught mother.

XVI

The sun withheld its usual splendor, and the day dawned pale and wan. Suzanne had risen early for a walk on the path encircling the hotel. The grass was still wet, and she was forced to confine her feet to the paved area. The crisp air was invigorating, promising a future molded more in line with fancy than with blatant fact. The next morning they would leave Hotel Riche, a departure she eagerly awaited. This day was for packing and for distribution of phone numbers, if that was all that could be done, but hopefully for a final and successful effort to extort commitment to Nancy from Philippe Juneau and to Betty from Harry Bellemore. Suzanne, however, was of little hope. She was cynical about the motives of her fellow men, although a sense of responsibility had caused her to work contrary to her expectations. Her own motives, she knew, could not bear close investigation. Her desire to be her own person and not merely a Margot appendage, dearly as she loved her family, had led her to violate, or at least stretch, her ideals of honesty and simplicity very thin in order to achieve the fulfillment of whatever freedom held for her by the satisfactory settlement of her sisters in marriage. Her mother had counted on and deserved her assistance in this endeavor, and until last night had not doubted the good sense of her offspring to encourage the younger girls into respectable paths and to check their at times excessive exuberance in social activities. Suzanne keenly felt her mother's disappointment with her. By day's end the failure of achieving unions with Juneau and Bellemore would put the stamp of finality on the loss of esteem Suzanne would suffer in her mother's judgment. This was the hardest loss to bear. The loss of her self-respect the night before was nothing to it; the guests meant nothing to her. Only the prospect of George Crump as stepfather had offered any possibility of good, of a wonderful mate for her mother and release from sisterly responsibilities for her. But the sight of her swinging from the chandelier could not have endeared the family to him. Whatever could have made her think it would? Only Harry Bellemore of the male foursome should have been witness to her disgrace and Betty's shining hour. But it was not to be. The crime had not succeeded.

It was in this frame of mind that she passed the tree by which she had faced down Harry Bellemore.

"Miss Margot."

She started at the sound of her name and the dreadfully familiar voice that had uttered it.

"Forgive me if I startled you," said Harry Bellemore, rising from the bench and blocking her path. "You are well, this morning?"

"Yes, thank you." He did not stand aside, however, and continued to look intently at her face. "I thought to get some morning air. It will probably rain before long." She would not look at him, but spoke, rather, to trees and blades of grass.

"Yes, rain is likely. May I walk with you?"

Suzanne's heart sank. "I would rather you didn't, Mr. Bellemore."

"I won't disturb you with talk. Won't you even allow me to breathe the same air as you? I promise not to inhale too deeply."

Suzanne was beside herself with frustration. How could she tell him that his very presence was disturbing to her.

"My purpose is not personal offense, but I would rather be alone."

"Then you are not well!"

"I am perfectly fine," she reiterated with just a touch of hysteria. "Must one be ill to seek fresh air and solitude?"

"I beg your pardon," he said feelingly, and stepped aside.

She took several steps forward before swinging around to face him. "What is it you want of me?" she cried.

"More than you are willing to give," he said somberly.

"I do not understand you."

"You do not wish to understand me. Have you no warmth, no spirit for anyone beyond your family? Are all joy, kindness, effort reserved for them alone? Must all else revolt you?"

"What do you know of my warmth and kindness?" she retorted.

Harry Bellemore was silent, his answer in no doubt.

Suzanne spoke strongly, though with faltering voice. "I am sorry if I've seemed rude or unkind to you. Such was not my purpose."

"So you say for a second time, Miss Margot. I consider your behavior last night offensive. Do you mean to tell me that you do not?"

"I am sorry you were placed in such danger, but your face is unmarked. You were foolish to attempt my rescue."

"Very foolish. Betty performed the part well."

"It was magnificent of her, genuine and sincere. Oh, I did not mean to imply—"

"It does not matter; I catch your drift. You would probably lie in the path of a locomotive if it would do Betty good. But it will not. Betty must make her own way; you cannot make it for her. I cannot admire you for trying. Perhaps I could in another situation; ordinarily I admire loyalty. But as its victim rather than its recipient I find it hard to appreciate. I see now that there is nothing I can do or say to win your love, except to oblige you by marrying Betty, but that would not satisfy the dictates of my heart, and I must satisfy mine as you are so determined to satisfy yours."

Suzanne was speechless, and the wonder on her face was interpreted by the man as horror at the tumult she had excited in him. He lowered his head as token of a formal bow.

"I will not detain you longer. Excuse me for having done so at all. The air is fresh and clean, perfumed by nature, not by glasses of scotch. Good morning."

Suzanne fled in the opposite direction, or rather her walk quickened. She did not rush, though there was no one to see, but she escalated her movements with fitting outward composure to brake her racing heart and the wild emotions flooding her mind, keeping them within the bounds of her body. Tears flowed down her cheeks, but she refused to recognize their existence by brushing them away. Upon entering the lobby, however, pride prompted her to wipe them rudely from her cheeks.

She knocked impatiently at the door of the family suite, impatiently opened it herself, and made a rapid entry to her room. There was not a glance at her mother sipping coffee with her sisters and not a word to her sisters, who stared at her wild looks and tear-stained face.

"*Now* what has she been doing?" came the long-suffering voice of Betty Margot.

Mrs. Margot knocked at the bedroom door. She waited a decent interval before turning the knob and entering. Suzanne lay on the bed, her face buried in the pillow, her body heaving with silent sobs. Her mother sat on the bed beside her and smoothed her daughter's hair. It had been many years since she had seen her eldest cry.

"Nothing can be worth those tears, my precious child. Will it help if I beg forgiveness for being so horrid to you last night?"

"Oh, Mother!" She turned her damp face toward her. "You were right. I was selfish and stupid; you have every right to hate me."

She cupped her daughter's face in her hands. "Hate you? My darling, I could never do that. You meant well, and you did not think of yourself inordinately. The last few years have been a trial with which I should not have burdened you. I've denied you a life of your own and you've taken it with admirable grace, and you take it still so. But you are a young woman, Suzanne, mature in your sense of responsibility and devotion to us all, but a young woman still. You are entitled to the joys of youth, and your heartaches should not be of my creating."

"Oh, Mother, that isn't so," she cried. "The burden was of my own making. Doing the right thing, the loving thing, should not be a burden. And what about *your* youth. You remain young, beautiful, and lovable and entitled to a private life even if your accomplishments as a mother are ignored. You certainly don't deserve to be trussed and hamstrung by ungrateful daughters lucky enough to have received so much love and old enough to understand the meaning of consideration.”

“I am entitled to no such thing. Mothers who think they are are never happy. I was at fault in not recognizing how great the pressure on you had become. But perhaps the events of this week had escalated the pressure beyond endurance?”

“The bathing suit incident was sheer agony.”

“Isn’t it more than that, Suzanne? We both have endured embarrassment from Betty before, and we know that there are other vacations, other parties, other men that lie in wait in her future.”

“And what a future! An endless parade of men endlessly lost. There must be an end to it, Mother.”

“So you have gone to extraordinary lengths to impose one. You know you can’t do that. The fact that you’ve tried in the face of this realization communicates another message.” Suzanne waited expectantly. “It had to be Harry Bellemore. It couldn’t be Barnesforth or Crump, or the Prince of Wales. It had to be the only man from whom you’ve felt danger. You’re in love with him, Suzanne. You don’t want to be, but you are. But my darling, love cannot be helped; it’s beyond effective control, like the first real day of spring and thunderstorms. It cannot be projected onto another, nor can sheer will power cause it to disappear. He has proposed to you, hasn’t he.”

“Yes, but the danger is past.”

“The pursuit is at an end; congratulations. You are a very foolish young woman.”

“I’ve worried so about the effect of last night on George. Did he phone this morning?”

“An arrangement for lunch made last night and a confirmation call this morning before I was barely out of bed.”

“That’s love!”

“That’s nonsense! And don’t change the subject. I can never condone your foolishness in rejecting a man whom you love and who loves you. Freedom without love? One may as well have food without teeth! When you feel you are ready for it love will not necessarily oblige. You are throwing realism into an ocean and idealism into a ditch. You are obstinate and you are wrong!”

"Your greater experience and discernment will not allow you to act so mulishly, I hope, and you will accept George Crump when he asks you to be his wife."

"I will not be drawn into such a conversation."

"He worships you."

"He feels secure with me."

"He feels happy and useful with you."

"Even working vacations are conducive to happiness, and the man has done a lot of good in this world without me."

"Then you respect and admire him. That is a start! You've always said that love grows in a well-founded marriage."

Mrs. Margot stood up abruptly. "Reconsider Harry Bellemore's proposal before it is too late. Look upon it as a piece of altruism, if you wish. After all, you can best forward Betty's future in such a marriage."

"As you can in a marriage to George Crump."

"Oh!" uttered Mrs. Margot, extending her hands upward in exasperation as she marched from the room.

Suzanne determined not to venture forth again that day. The possibility of another encounter with Harry Bellemore was not to her liking, and the man seemed to be everywhere. Betty was persuaded by the imagined re-interest of Harry Bellemore to appear, tantalizing of dress and modest in demeanor, where that gentleman might see and approach her. Nancy was off for a day with Philippe. Suzanne watched them all leave with relief. A vacation in her room was what she most wanted now, but solitude led to thinking, and thinking was worse than useless; it was depressing. To keep herself from contemplating the dispiriting results of her officious tampering with life, she resorted to the radio. News of a world beyond match-making should have reduced the past week to insignificance, but she had never been one to whom survival was dependent on someone else's grief. Commercials, formerly accepted and ignored, now gained dimension as irritants, and only Handel provided relief. With beauty and order she was soothed. Her mind and heart were placated, joined, and soon at peace, which made packing a mechanical task, divorced from unpleasant experiences. But Handel was succeeded by

Beethoven, and troubling thoughts made a play for ascendance; the mind would not be denied. Since fresh reading material was not at hand, she decided on an immediate visit to the library. It had been designed with privacy in mind, with nooks and deeply upholstered, high-backed chairs with embracing arms.

The library was empty. If the gray promise of morning were fulfilled and the library became populated, she would withdraw books at the reception desk and return with them to her room. She settled in with a favorite, *Mont St. Michel & Chartres,* and was soon lost to reflections of another age. But parallels began to suggest themselves and she replaced the book on the shelf. She did not want the mental gymnastics of philosophy or the unraveling of lessons unlearned from history. She had decided on a guide to London when she was tapped on the elbow. A young boy's imploring eyes met hers.

"Please, Miss, could you help me find these magazines?" He showed her a list of four. "We don't seem to have them, but there's a big tip if we do."

"I'm afraid you forgo the tip. You might advise the guest to purchase them in the shop in the lobby. They're probably for sale there."

"They are, but—well, ten dollars is a lot to lose."

"Yes, it is. But promise of a tip for what is unavailable is promise of no tip at all." With London in hand she returned to her seat, the boy following.

"Would you be interested in the magazines, Miss?"

She narrowed her eyes at the young face. "If you want me to buy them and lend them to you, I will not. They are the kind of magazines that a woman who wants them should at least have the decency to buy herself."

"I'll give you half the take."

"When I get to London they'll deport me for bribery."

"I'll take all the blame; I'm too young to stand trial."

"Do your parents know what you are doing?"

"They work here. I help them out when they're too busy."

"Go to the shop and thumb through those magazines. I doubt if you'll want to deliver them to the woman."

"It's not right to read magazines you don't buy. Dealers have to make a living."

"I'm glad your standards are high. Let that be a comfort to you in lieu of the ten dollars."

"But she's too sick to leave her room. Please help me, lady."

"If I get those magazines for you, I may very well get sick, too. Will you then deliver reading material to me?"

"All you want, for no tip at all!"

Her curiosity was piqued. "Have you seen this woman?"

"No, Miss, but I've gotten her things before. She really is sick though; her voice never sounds the same. Rotten luck getting sick on vacation."

"Perhaps several women share the room."

"Oh, no, just the lady and her husband."

"A husband! And you've never been the least bit curious to see what this lady with all her requests looks like?"

The boy shrugged. "She doesn't open the door. Her husband orders the meals and I leave them outside the door. She must be an elegant lady, though. When a woman has an accent she usually is."

"Well, you will have to ask the elegant lady for money to buy the magazines and take your chance with the tip. If she wants them badly enough she will pay. It would be preferable to having her husband buy them for her."

"He might not understand."

"But for ten dollars, you do?"

"Absolutely."

She laughed. "Then this little errand will not corrupt you, but I will not assist you."

"If I were a Frenchman I could persuade you."

"When you become one come back about this." He grimaced. "I'm sorry," she said sincerely.

"I'll ask for the money," he said resignedly. "It's either that or she'll have to ask the tall, stiff husband or do without."

He was nearly out the door when Suzanne's cry stopped him. "Wait a minute! The husband is French?"

"Yes, didn't I say so?"

"Why do you call him stiff?"

"His posture; he must have been in the army or something. Lady, I've got to go."

"Are there many Frenchmen registered in the hotel?"

"There aren't any I know of, except him."

"Well, we should certainly help the French; they did so much for us during the American Revolution. I'll buy those magazines on condition that you allow me to deliver them."

"Uh-uh. That's my job. She won't open the door anyway."

"You can tell her they're a gift, not a loan. Your tip should increase."

"And what do you get out of it?"

"Satisfaction. I won't keep the money, I promise."

"Well, I don't know—but, all right. I'll phone and say I'm having them sent right up. Got a pencil? I'll write the room number."

The sense of danger was extraordinary. It put her own position on related matters in the shade. Philippe Juneau was with Nancy. Then who were the women in his room, for women there assuredly were. She bought the magazines, averting her eyes from those of the salesman, and without perusing them in the least headed in the direction of the mystery.

The shock of Juneau's perfidy and the embarrassment of her reading purchase quickly gave way to anger. She was angry at the carpeting in the lobby, angry at the elevator button, angry at Juneau, but most of all angry at herself. She had suspected, and strongly, that something was the matter with the man and had not warned Nancy. Never mind that actual proof had been lacking, it had been her duty to prevent harm of any kind to her sister, not acquiesce to it. The fact that she had informed her mother of her doubts and attempted to align Nancy with Derek Barnesforth flew from her head. Her failure in all its nakedness confronted her, and she was not in a forgiving mood. There was the actuality of the shut door. Two, three, heaven knew how many women who had no quarrel with Suzanne Margot, who doubtless had never heard of Nancy Margot, and who were probably not a party to duplicity were on the other side of this barrier. Strange women surely, but a case apart from the callousness

at hand. Marriage! The unthinkableness of it! Was the man propos-
ing to juggle monogamy with a harem? No amount of wealth entitled him to that, not, at any rate, with a Margot. Anger yielded to
astonishment and determination. Suzanne placed the magazines on
the table beside the door, knocked on that massive obstacle twice,
and announced the presence of the magazines. She walked deliberately and heavily toward the elevator, kicked off her shoes, and sped
in stockinged feet back down the corridor. She flattened her back
against the wall, and when many minutes later the upper torso of a
woman curled itself around the door's edge and a hand reached for
the magazines, Suzanne was able to grab the hand, struggle with it,
force it back into the room still in her grasp, and kick the door shut
behind her.

"You have no right to come in like this," exclaimed the young
woman in well-schooled English. She was about Suzanne's age, dark-
haired, sensuous, and scared. She massaged her hand.

"I didn't mean to hurt you. I only want information from you—
and your friend."

The woman absorbed her stern gaze. "I have nothing to tell
you; get out of here!"

"You know I won't," Suzanne said evenly. "Where is your friend?
Under the bed, in a dry tub with today's newspaper?"

"You're out of your mind; you've got the wrong room. I insist
you leave immediately!"

Suzanne lifted the telephone receiver. "Shall I dial Security for
you?"

"No! No. We meant no harm to you; we're no threat to you,
really. Why won't you go away! You say you don't want to hurt us,
but you will hurt us if you stay. No man of substance will hire us; our
reputations will be ruined." Her voice shook.

"If you answer my questions, your reputation for clandestine
responsibility will remain intact and I will leave."

"What you're asking is unfair. Our standards won't permit us to
respond."

"Well, if I should tell Mr. Juneau of our little conversation, I'm
sure he will appreciate the courage you showed in assuming the entire

responsibility for discussing the matter with me instead of involving anyone else."

"Discussing? I've not been discussing anything with you, and there's no one else to involve."

"Then Mr. Juneau should not object to your having told me that you know him, that your profession is prostitution—of the most honorable kind—that you are 'we' and that I have been wronged by your behavior. Haven't you said these things?"

"I—I can't talk without Evyette's permission." She lifted the lid of a huge war chest at the foot of the king-size bed.

"You are all thoughtfulness," said Evyette sarcastically, stepping out of the container.

"I'm not about to get the shaft from you for speaking out."

"I want to know why you are here."

The two women looked at each other. Then the dark-haired one sighed and got immediately to the point. Without his back brace Mr. Juneau suffered excruciating pain from a skiing accident suffered many years ago. He divested himself of the brace during intercourse. The excitement and exertion caused him to scream like a madman from pain. This behavior unnerved the ladies, resulting in temporary frigidity and the wish never to see him again. In consequence of this, he had hired the two of them, who had come highly recommended by another gentleman, to wait on his pleasure and mute his cries. Thus, the participants were willing and understanding, the neighbors were spared the shrieks, and Mr. Juneau's needs were satisfied. And that was all—truly. It was an act of mercy they were performing.

Suzanne recalled that his failed marriages had followed the skiing mishap. "This, then, was the source of the 'incompatibility' that led to his divorces?"

"Yes, a woman has to be strong, in complete control of her emotions to bear this. Evyette and I are strong."

And well-paid, she thought. "This does not account for your presence here. Does Mr. Juneau have so little self-control that he cannot curb his desire for a week?"

"We're no desire; we're a need. Since we have been with him—how long has it been Jeanne, nine months?—we've become a daily ritual. We are his drugs."

"As medicinal properties you are undoubtedly invaluable, unless Mr. Juneau marries again."

"He talks about it, but he would be a fool to do that. Who would stay married to a sexual cripple?"

"I thought you said his back—"

"Oh, yes, but he's not all that good, and a rag in the mouth is a turn-off to a woman who's not a pro," she said matter-of-factly.

"And you detect no appeal Mr. Juneau might have for a woman beyond sex?"

"Well, there is his money, and the possibility for a bedroom life besides his, but only a hard-boiled woman could make do with only the money, and only a clever woman could manage another sex life. Mr. Juneau is very jealous, and he's very sensitive about his manhood, as you might expect. His second wife found that out."

"Beat her badly, did he?"

"Very, but it cost him a bundle. He's not a stupid man; he won't marry again. You his girlfriend?"

"I'm an interested party."

Evyette laughed. "Better that way. He's not for you. He's not for anyone but us." She laughed again.

Jeanne spoke anxiously. "You will keep this between the three of us?"

"Woman's honor," said Suzanne. "Enjoy the magazines." "Thanks. We've got to make a living like anyone else. Wait. Here's ten dollars for the kid. You promised, remember?"

XVII

t was 2 o'clock in the afternoon and the whereabouts of her family were unknown. A phone call to their suite confirmed that no one was there. There was a period of legwork in store, but what she would say at its completion was not clear to her. Nancy could not marry Juneau, that much she knew, but it would be unnecessary to say once Nancy became acquainted with the conduct of his life. However, how to say it with the least pain to her sister was what occupied her thoughts. With sanctioned but spurious reasoning, Nancy had convinced herself of the merits of the match and begun to absorb it into her emotions. Suzanne had promised the duo in Juneau's room silence on the matter, but what was a promise to them compared to the duty due her sister? Her mother was used to the vagaries of romantic fortune and would, after the initial shock and disappointment, chart other plans to capture other men. But the breach of faith rankled, and for a fleeting moment she hoped that Juneau would be honest enough in his formal proposal to include an account of his habits. The hope was a passing one.

At 4 o'clock a weary Suzanne went back to their suite to await the return of her clan. Betty bounded in first, danced around the room twice, and burst into speech.

"Guess whom I've been with!"

Suzanne suffered a brief palpitation. "I've no idea," she lied.

"With Charles, lovely Charles!" She danced again.

"I thought you found Charles dull."

"I met him on the path to the lake where I was going to meditate, and we walked there together and met Nancy and Philippe, and we walked and talked. At least Charles did. He knows so much! Nancy had all the spirit of her spouse-to-be, who was as stiff and boring as usual. But Charles just sparkled and talked about everything and knew about everything. Nancy gave me such looks! I had a wonderful time!"

"Has Philippe proposed yet?"

"They didn't say. He may be waiting for the moon and the stars to bless his proposal. What do you think of me and Charles?"

"Do you want to marry him?"

"Of course not. I can't marry every man who wants me."

"You could take them one at a time."

"You're very nasty today, Zanny; what's the matter?"

"Charles has spoken privately to both my sisters and my mother and has ignored me."

"At your age you should really be more serious. I'll be in the shower."

Suzanne marched up and down the room, revolving the problem on her mind until the telephone rang.

"Company halt! Is there any way I can help?"

"Where's Mother?"

"On her way up. What's the trouble?"

Could she, should she trust George? What did he know of the matter? Would he betray the confidence of a friend?

"The trouble is I'm a creature of habit. I'll stop walking. Thank you for asking."

"Hold on. Are you sure there's no problem? I can come up if you'd like. Ask your mother to call me about this when she gets in."

Suzanne could not resist a smile. "I'll tell her."

"Yes, tell her—tell her—tell her I—tell her I want to help, genuinely, sincerely, with all my heart. You will do that, won't you?" he asked piteously. "Just tell her—" His voice trailed off.

"I'll tell her George, with all *my* heart."

"God bless you! I've been such a fool. Tell her." And he rang off.

So Suzanne was prepared for the entry of her mother, flushed and upset.

"George called."

"Is that Betty in the shower? Where's Nancy? They haven't finished packing; I hope you have, at least. We must be ready to leave by 6 o'clock. We'll breakfast on the plane."

"He heard me pacing, believed there was a problem, and asked me to tell you to call him about it."

"Our problems are none of George Crump's business!" she erupted. "What problem?"

"He apologized for being a fool."

"Which part of his inane monologue was he referring to? But it doesn't matter. Where is my jewelry case? I can't seem to find anything anymore." Suzanne pointed to the desktop. "Thank you, dear. We'll have dinner in. Make out a menu like a good child. My silk scarf has vanished. Where did you say Nancy was?"

"With Philippe. Betty in the company of Charles tortured her unmercifully with that fact when they met her and Philippe by the lake."

"Nancy may have dinner out."

"No, she mustn't Mother, at least not with Philippe."

"Why not with Philippe?"

"She can't marry him, Mother. He's got problems that are beyond Nancy's ability to cope with; he won't make a satisfactory husband."

"What's this? I insist on details immediately."

"It's a sex problem, Mother," she said delicately.

"They've all got that!" Her mother's eyes blazed indignantly. "But he wants to marry her, doesn't he? Or doesn't he!"

"It seems he does, but his behavior during the—uh—performance requires tons of patience and understanding. His two marriages failed because of this, and Nancy won't be able to manage, won't want to manage. She loves Charles and she should marry Charles. He'll be a somebody some day and, if I judge rightly, he'll always be a somebody, regardless, to Nancy."

"On what is this judgment based, this accusation against Philippe, this assumption about the staying power of your sister, this gratuitous defense of Charles?"

"Don't be angry, Mother. I want her well-married as much as you do, but this arrangement won't work. Philippe is a marital misfit. I pledged not to reveal the story, but there is no doubt; I saw the evidence with my own eyes."

"Is this the problem George wants me to call him about?"

"I didn't tell him what the problem was, but I'm afraid I was pacing again."

"The gall of the man! I urged him to speak well of Nancy to Philippe, in case he should falter in his ardor for her. He wouldn't do it! He mentioned this relative, that friend for her, but the most available, the most promising he brushed aside. I was justifiably angry. I would have none of his role-playing, his game-playing with my daughter's future. I accused him of insincerity."

"Oh, Mother, you didn't!"

"I did! And I don't regret it! He said he had no art of manipulation, that he would do all for me because he wanted all from me. I've never been so furious with anyone. I don't clearly remember what I said. The man's a lecher, a sex maniac of the worst sort, the kind who preys upon women in the guise of gentility, meekness, and good deeds. I detest him!"

It was now her mother's turn to pace, and Suzanne let her. She remembered the deaf ear she had given Harry Bellemore, the fury she had felt toward him, and the consequences thereof. After a while she spoke. "George meant well, Mother, but you couldn't know that. He didn't want to betray his friend by offering you details, but he didn't want Nancy to involve herself in a mistake. He's spoken little to Nancy, so the consideration, the compliment was to you."

"Compliment!" Mrs. Margot scoffed. "Interest in my body is a compliment?"

Suzanne rejected both flippancy and the flattering truth. "You say you felt justified in expecting help from George. Knowing what men are, why did you feel this way?"

"I was an old fool; I made a mistake. Your mother does make mistakes, you know."

"You are neither old, nor a fool, and I'm not sure this judgment was a mistake."

"If you are going to advance that stupid theory again, I will not hear it!" And she stormed to her room and slammed the door behind her.

Suzanne could not remember when she had last seen her mother so angry or so forgetful. Juneau had been eclipsed from her mind and sense had vanished. There could be no doubt. She was wildly in love with George Crump. Before she could do little more than rejoice at this, Nancy entered, grinning broadly, and triumphantly announced "He's proposed! The richest, handsomest, most eligible man in the world has proposed to me!"

The extravagance was not lost on Suzanne. "You will have to learn French, business science to run the enormous household and agriculture—his roots, you know."

"I'll have plenty of time to learn—weeks and weeks. He's everything I've ever wanted. Only I haven't said yes yet. Not that I have any doubts, but a little agony never made a man care less."

Suzanne was about to speak when Betty, tying her robe about her, entered. Her reception of the proposal did not match Nancy's telling of it.

"You needn't put on such long faces, both of you. At least Mama will be happy for me. Is she in her room?"

"She's resting—exhaustion. Leave her be for a while." She was reluctant to speak of Juneau in front of Betty. "Is he calling for you here before dinner?"

"No, I'm meeting him in the dining room at 7 o'clock."

"Wouldn't he be delightfully surprised if you called for *him* at his room, say 6:30?"

"Zanny, what a good idea!"

"Propriety, propriety," warned Betty.

"We're practically engaged," Nancy fired back.

"You mean you're not engaged yet?"

"Are you?"

"Girls, please. I'll help you dress, Nancy."

"The world is full of wonders. Our Zanny, servant to the rich and famous. Even I wouldn't stoop that far."

"You wouldn't have to," Nancy shot back as she ushered Suzanne into her room and locked the door.

But there was little Suzanne could say to convince; she had tried before. Only the sight of those two in his room would convey the awkward truth. She gingerly mentioned his former marriages and their dissolution, cultural differences between them, everything that might engender problems. Oblique glances at her sister assured her that these seeds had not taken root. Obstacles were to be swept away by their love. Her disenchantment would be sudden and sharp. Suzanne sighed aloud, and Nancy came to her and hugged her much as the older had often done for her. Nancy understood, she thought, and she determined to work for the romantic happiness of her beloved sibling.

Mrs. Margot, appearing weary and spent, quit her room in time to see her youngest depart. Eye communication with her eldest assured her that the Juneau matter had been tackled, and so trusting was she of her eldest child that Nancy's high spirits, obviously intended to unsettle Betty, did not persuade her otherwise.

In the elevator Nancy's spirits underwent a change, and by the time she exited they had definitely flagged. The romance associated with Philippe Juneau was the romance of expectation; the reality loomed awesome and frightening. It was with mixed feelings that she faced the door to his room, for in addition to forebodings pressing strongly upon her, was the sight of a cart like the one that would be parked outside the family suite awaiting the supper dishes. Juneau had planned a private supper, Zanny had known, had feigned ignorance, had led her to it. Her sister's sanction caused her spirits to fall completely. Somehow she had counted on her opposition. She longed for people, crowds of them, mobs of them, and gobs and gobs of food. She would hurry to the dining room, the only arrangement she had been party to, and await him there. The temptation was great, but something kept her from it. What she had been taught to cherish lay beyond the doorway, and fear could not so quickly dislodge the accumulated learning of years. She steadied her thoughts with this and knocked on the door. There was no response, not then nor many knocks later. Insecurity gave way to worry and she knocked vigorously. She called Philippe's name to no avail. She walked to the hall phone and dialed his room with the same result. She dialed again. "Security?"

"Don't do that." George Crump stood tieless, shirttails out, at the entrance to his room.

She replaced the receiver. "Is he all right?"

"He's as usual, but he cannot come to the door now."

She looked at him curiously. "How do you know that?"

"Habit."

"Oh, but you must tell me all about his habits. A good wife must know everything that can make her husband comfortable."

"I would rather we didn't talk in the corridor. Come in."

"Philippe would never understand *that*. Tell me here."

George hesitated. "Philippe has not told you about his guests, then. He has guests. They are important to him and he feeds them well. He needs them for his—back. His back is a serious problem."

"They are doctors, then?"

"No, laymen. He's sensitive about the problem and he prefers to be silent about it. You must ask him about his guests."

"Oh, I shall. They sound intriguingly mysterious."

"Is your mother well?"

"Why, yes. Was it likely she would become ill in the half hour since you last saw her?"

"No, I suppose not. Send her my—best wishes. I'll see her and your sisters at dinner, I hope."

"I think not. They're eating in."

"I see." He shuffled his feet. "Philippe will be out soon. He will be unhappy knowing you were waiting in the corridor."

"I thought he had planned a private supper for us in his room, as a surprise. I should have guessed he couldn't do anything as romantically ordinary as that."

"No. Uh, excuse me." Several minutes after he heard her footsteps fade away, he opened his door and knocked on Philippe's. "It's George. It's all right. I must speak to you."

The door opened immediately, testifying to an ear at the door.

"You can't marry the girl, Phil."

"Thank you for keeping Security away, but yes, I can."

"She's just a child; she will never put up with this."

"She's loyal, malleable, and good-natured. She'll meet the challenge, revel in the challenge. My wives are my business George. She'll have everything—"

"Even the truth? Will you tell her the truth before you marry her?"

"I'll tell her."

George mooned about hoping that in some secluded area of the hotel he would find her. His initial attempt to appropriate the Bellemore style had not suited. The belief that the lady was available for transient use had silenced his sense of virtue and freed his romantic impulses from their usual restraint. That she needed him and would feel beholden in a manner congenial to him and not unfamiliar to herself had hastened the eclipse of his reason. And now it was too late to revoke the excitement she had elicited, the joy he had known in being needed. With the coming of truth, virtue had resumed its reign within him. For him the escapade was over, as for her it had never even begun. He felt dejected, desolate, and friendless. There was no one to comfort him, to sympathize with him, or make the pain, the memory, the woman disappear. Harry had been aloof and unresponsive to his hints for consolation, if not help, and his mother, who had made some pointed and unflattering remarks about the lady in question, could be expected to attempt to erase Eleanor Margot from his heart with a violence at least equal to that with which she had gained entry to it. It was in such a state that he ran into Nancy Margot. Quite literally, he knocked her sideways as they passed each other at the garden entrance to the hotel. He begged forgiveness and was accorded a breathless one, more breathless than the incident required. He inquired if she had dined, and she nodded affirmatively.

"Are you going to marry him?" he asked softly.

"Why should that concern you?"

"I would rather neither of you was unhappy."

"If you are referring to those guests you worry so about, I can take care of that little matter," she snapped.

"Little? Those—"

"Those whores are nothing to him, nothing to me, nothing to anybody of consequence, Mr. Crump. When I marry Philippe I will be the women of the house—all of them! I'm quite capable of handling all roles, so I'll thank you not to upset yourself about my life. I'm sure your mother would agree." She tried to walk past him.

"*Your* mother would not. You will not be able to dislodge those two. His behavior will disgust you. You will learn to despise the agony of the ritual; you will learn to hate him. And the hired help will win; you will gladly yield your place by his side to them. He will make allowances for his medicine, but he will not tolerate your infidelity, and you will have the choice of living as a married virgin or divorcing him for as large a settlement as threats will produce. Is that what you really want?"

Nancy was beside herself with frustration and anger. "You are a jealous, hateful man! All those women—"

"Two, Nancy, just two, the same two. Didn't he tell you? He promised me he would tell you."

"You're lying! You're trying to frighten me! Well, you can't. I'm the only one he wants, the only one he needs. All your spiteful words can't change the truth!"

"Would you like to see the truth? They are in his room now. See them, speak to them, and judge for yourself."

"I don't believe you!"

"You don't have to believe me, or does the truth frighten you? If it does, if my mere words frighten you, then there isn't a prayer for your marriage to Philippe."

"I'm not afraid of anything," she hurled defiantly.

"We'll see."

Nancy, face flushed and perspiring, flew into their suite as into a rage. "I'm going to marry Philippe," she announced, and slammed herself into her room.

An eager Betty, more desirous of leaving the confines of the suite than partaking vicariously of her sister's love life, was given the run of the hotel, and Eleanor Margot and Suzanne marched into Nancy's room. Only Suzanne's admittance of an interview with Philippe's women elicited the hair-raising details of consummation in progress upon Nancy's surprise entry into Juneau's sanctuary via the connecting door from George's room. Vindictive words were uttered, followed by a loud argument, followed by a reasonably controlled discussion among the four of them, George having been relegated to perdition, although he refused to leave until the confrontation was over. With tears streaming down her cheeks, Nancy vowed loyalty to Philippe, defended him with passion from all attack, and affirmed her readiness to marry him that minute. Mother and daughter reasoned with her in vain and quit her room in consternation.

"She is going to marry Juneau, and all because of George's clumsy interference. We could have persuaded her otherwise, but no! He had to come blundering into what's none of his affair, stomping on her dreams, ripping decency to pieces! I am going to make my feelings very clear to him and right now!"

Suzanne blocked her way. "You will do nothing of the sort. His motives were all you could wish. He did it as much for you as for Nancy."

"Upsetting my daughter to such an extent that he drives her into the arms of the worst man she could marry is doing something for me? Step out of my way!"

"You want to see him again, don't you?" Suzanne asked desperately.

"I never want to see him again, after this!" The door was vigorously exercised once more.

Suzanne threw herself into a chair and watched glumly as the last rays of sunshine struggled through the window. The chase, the struggle, the hope, the disillusion would be forgotten and yield to others like it. The hunt had failed; it had not been designed for success, only for torture, torture of an exquisitely amenable sort for Betty, of varying degrees of acceptability for Nancy and her mother, and of excruciating rawness for herself. Worst of all it had become a habit, a stultifying routine. No marriage would result, no marriage should result from such connivance. Nancy, upon second thought, would reject Juneau; she was no fool and she loved Charles. It was the world of expectations turned upside down—her mother and George, Nancy and Charles, she and Harry—or perhaps turned right side up, despite shrewd maneuvers and secret plans to the contrary. If only her mother would marry George; if only Harry would stop intruding on her dreams. The perfect mate—dashing, handsome, ardent, secure— was not to be the mate for her. Habit. She had spent so many years in an attempt to get others mated that the idea of yielding herself had formed no part of her fantasy. The reality of love and affection meant responsibility and sacrifice, and she had had enough of those. Marriage? In some distant corner of her life it lay reachable only after a period of tranquillity and the dimming of adventures past. She was not chaste enough in mind to contemplate marriage now. She was not ready for Harry Bellemore yet. Would such as he be waiting for her when she was? She was tempted to swear at the perverseness of fate, but she had given that up long ago. Habit again. She was glad when Pedro wheeled in dinner. For a while, at least, food and the waiter's good fortune could occupy her mind.

"Thank you, Pedro. How is your wife?"

"She is fine. We wait." He collected his tip and waited. "Your last night I ask the food be cooked just right. Is good?"

"I'm sure it is, but if I lift the lids now the food will get cold."

"One little lift, it will stay hot. Not to worry."

"Thank you, Pedro, and good-bye." She took his hand in hers. He held it in his for a moment longer than necessary or proper, and she noticed his eyes for the first time, large, familiar. "Your wife will be fine," she echoed. "You will be a father soon, and for that you have my warmest wishes for success—and luck." And ever so gently she maneuvered him into the corridor and closed the door. She reflected that the only peace of the evening might be that of the moment, and she decided to eat in the relative calm of it, tumbled feelings notwithstanding. She quickly lifted lids to find her salad, and an exclamation of surprise escaped her when she did. Shielded from the chicken and cherry tomatoes lay a miniature silver rose with petals meticulously shaped, glittering on white damask. She ran to the door and shouted for Pedro, still visible down the corridor. He approached hesitantly, and she ushered him back into the suite.

"This rose has been mistakenly delivered."

"No, Madam, there is no mistake. I can say no more. You guess, maybe?"

"It belongs with the broiled salmon, then," she said frantically.

"No, Madam, for you. It makes you unhappy?"

"I cannot accept it; you must take it back."

"No, Madam, I take nothing back; it is for you."

"But I cannot accept it, don't you understand?"

"It is a gift."

"It is not a gift!" she cried.

"He seems a good man. Why do you hate him so?"

"I don't hate him. Oh, this will not do! You must take it away."

"Maybe gold. If he loves you, maybe gold?"

"No, silver is perfect, beautiful. You don't understand. It will not do!"

"You are right; I do not understand. It is perfect, but you refuse it."

She snatched the rose from the damask and thrust it at him, but he turned abruptly toward the door and would have opened it had not Mrs. Margot done so suddenly, hurtling it into his face.

"Oh, forgive me, I—Mr. Bellemore!"

Half his mustache clung to the door, and red-faced from embarrassment and the sudden bang, he pulled the other half from his face. "I'm sorry, Suzanne. My appearance has been deceptive, but my feelings have been genuine. Try to understand my desperation as I'm sure your mother does. Mrs. Margot, I beg your daughter's hand in marriage."

Suzanne was so choked with his presumption that only indignation gave her a voice. "Out! Or you'll get the back of *my* hand! Cheat, lie, grab what strikes your fancy, what stimulates you to rise to dizzying heights of vulgarity, but not with me! You make a mockery of hard-working people with real joys, sorrows, and needs. You are not a human being I care to look on further. You are sham human, a delusion of the noxious air in this hotel. Get out and take your masquerade elsewhere!"

"Suzanne, you go too far!"

"No, Mother, nothing I could say would be enough to express my revulsion at the sight of him—sham, fake, seducer!"

Harry Bellemore left without another word. From twenty feet behind him he heard her still. "And take your canned romance with you!" An object thudded to the carpet at his heels. He did not choose to look.

Eleanor Margot sat beside her daughter, now sobbing bitterly on her bed. "We never should have come here. I meant well, but I was mistaken. How could I have known that things would turn out so? A sick son-in-law to-be and my darling Suzanne crying more in one week than in her whole life. So much effort and so little satisfaction from it all." She dwelt wistfully on George Crump and sighed. "Ages too young," she murmured. "And Harry Bellemore, gay blade supreme, falls sensibly in love with my foolish daughter. My fault. I've made men a torment for you. All the responsibility all those years."

Suzanne raised her head from the coverlet. "No, Mother, you are not to blame. It's my way, my stupid, senseless, stubborn way, and it always will be. I won't have you blaming yourself." And she burst into tears again.

"There, there, darling. We'll soon be in our own home and in our own world. How I wish we were now!"

XVIII

Suzanne creased her forehead at the figures on the paper. At the office in the morning she would satisfy herself of their accuracy by a quick check on the calculator. She disdained owning one herself. It enfeebled the mind, made it dependent, and was, overall, a bad thing. Her room was a reflection of her orderly and active mind. The desk was uncluttered and the floor unencumbered with piles of anything. The ceiling-high book shelves lining two walls boasted double layers of well-thumbed books on a variety of subjects seemingly unconnected with the practice of law, and only the cotton lace curtains and the oval pile rug hinted at more than function, knowledge, and restraint. A breeze blew through the window from the garden beyond, still green and gratifying, but the otherwise quiet, final throes of summer were matched by the stillness in the house. Her sisters were off shopping with their mother, Nancy for a trousseau and Betty for a rise of spirits, which had sagged notably since the vacation of a month before. She had taken to impatience with them all and to special cruelty to Nancy, and Mrs. Margot had decided that a wardrobe and the expectations it produced would mitigate the pain and possibly precipitate the desired conquest. Figures throbbed in Suzanne's head, but the stillness of the house was a congenial antidote. She did not object to taking work home. The fabric of work and private life was, in essence, a seamless one, and pretending otherwise was foolish. Besides, she liked her work and the feeling of control and direction it enabled her to impose on her days.

She put the papers in her briefcase and pulled a volume from the shelf. Then she reached into the bottom drawer of a chest. The movement disturbed a silver object. Removing a shawl, she took it and the book into the living room. Cords of wood were on order, so the small fireplace in the corner remained unlit, but Suzanne gazed with satisfaction at it, her imagination supplying the harmless illusion of warmth. Reading made her oblivious of all else until the doorbell broke into her thoughts. She had surely dozed off and imagined it, imagined that Harry Bellemore had stood on the doorstep looking subdued and proper in a blue suit. Surely she had reluctantly invited him into the house after warning him of the absence of anyone he might care to speak to. He had made no mention of their final meeting, but instead had displayed a letter from George to her mother to be delivered with a personal explanation from himself. But the hot coffee burning her throat was real, and the man facing her in her own domain, away from the social arena was, too.

"Mr. Crump is well, I hope?"

"Quite well. And your family?"

"Also well. And his mother?" she asked pointedly.

"Not so well. She is suffering from sibling insurrection and even refused the gift of a debt-free weekend in Monte Carlo crying 'bribery.' George will not ask again."

"Is the nature of this insurrection contained in the letter to my mother?"

"Yes; you guess the meaning. All his friends have found him impossible for thinking of her. She is in the boardroom with him, on the golf course, at every meal. The event that will restore normality is marriage. He is past all else. I never expected to be a tool toward such a goal, but I haven't been too well myself." He looked at her intensely, and she dropped her eyes.

"On holiday the atmosphere, the very air plays tricks on the mind. Mr. Crump may still be under its spell."

"George has been subject to sudden enthusiasms which dissolved as suddenly, but he has never been subject to spells. His commitment will not change." He hesitated. "You know something of that, I believe. You are committed to family and feeling. There is little likelihood of change, I would suppose?"

Suzanne fought to disguise the rapid beating of her heart. Could he still have any interest in her? His manner was so proper, so respectful. It was the rose.

"It's the rose you've also come for, Mr. Bellemore, isn't it? I'm embarrassed that I've kept it this long; I did not mean to."

"I had hoped that you did mean to keep it. I had hoped…There is no one else I care to give it to, but in another forty-four years, when I may, I'd hardly make a suitable rosenkavalier."

"Even now you are twenty-seven years too late. You cannot pass as a boy of 17, though next year I shall assume the age of the marschallin. Do you think my behavior will pass for hers as well?"

"Her fears will not color them. You will be your own marschallin. Marie-Theres would wish herself you."

"Then she would be a foolish woman for, although only for a short time, she had her rosenkavalier."

Harry Bellemore sprang to his feet, his eyes aglow. "I've just dropped twenty-seven years!"

"I've been such a fool, and yet—"

"No! You've thought enough for now. After our marriage I guarantee you leisure to think all you wish."

"I derive so much satisfaction from my career that—"

"Then I guarantee you as little leisure as you please. My guarantees are flexible, the flexibility of a madman, but sanity holds no appeal to me if it deprives me of you. But please, I beg you, say little and think little until I am 17."

"And I am 32, and a bonafide Strauss marschallin."

"I love you."

"Yes." And the words she could not say for newness he did not demand. "Why did you give me a whole, wretched month of waiting?"

"I had no reason to hope you had changed your mind until your mother's letter arrived yesterday."

"Mother wrote to you?" She blushed.

"She wrote that the rose was mine, and if I wanted it back it was safely stored at the bottom of one of your bedroom drawers. That gave me hope, and I could not rest until I knew. You may have your career, your freedom, whatever you like, but I hope you won't object to my dropping in on legal meetings, research sessions, bubble baths to say I love you. I've become very much like George, you see."

Suzanne blushed again. "I've liked George from the start."

"From the start? I'd be inclined to be jealous if I hadn't the vision of your drawer to relieve me. Is there a chance for George?"

"Mother has been impossible on the subject. She would like to be persuaded, I think, but she is more ingrained in habit than I. If only George had come himself!"

"So I told him."

The front door opened to the bustle of packages and vocal uproar.

"Grab the hat box!"

"What happened to my gloves? Have you got them, Nancy?"

"You're dropping my gown!"

"It's falling! I've got it, I've got it!"

And in the midst of the women and the commotion stood George Crump beaming, his head barely showing above the boxes in his arms. "Hello everybody—Suzanne, Harry."

The packages were tumbled onto the sofa.

The bride-to-be gushed. "George was a godsend with his car and his chauffeur. He didn't even stop to choose the hat he came to Radmor's to buy!"

Suzanne looked questioningly at her mother from whom these words would ordinarily have emanated.

"So kind," she merely added, busying herself with hanging jackets and sweaters in the hall closet.

George Crump dispensed with his sacrifice with the wave of a hand. "I had the least trouble of you all. I didn't have the bother of trying on the contents of these boxes."

"Such patience," cooed Nancy.

"George says gloves are the very thing for elegant affairs," and Betty tore into the box containing hers and held aloft the perishable satin that Suzanne had not yet seen and that Nancy, in high conviviality, did not object to admiring once again.

Mrs. Margot disappeared, coffee the excuse. Suzanne followed her. Her mother's face was red from more than the bustling.

"What a coincidence that George should appear at Radmor's, to buy one of their ugly hats no less, when we do. Incredible that he should even have been aware of the existence of the store."

"Mother, you can try to appreciate the favor for itself."

"I'm six years his senior!"

"Not in sense."

"Sense? You talk of sense? You call your rejection of Harry Bellemore sense? You keep his silver rose hidden in your drawer—yes, I looked and I'm not sorry—and you deny yourself and him happiness in spite of it. It makes me angry just to think of it."

"Then, I reflect you, Mother. George is a darling man, even without his money and position and in spite of his mother, and you enjoy his company, yet you will have none of it. Of course, if you set me a different example."

"It's not the same; Harry is thirteen years older than you."

"Older by more than a decade. *Too* old."

"You won't convince me."

"As you won't convince me. Only our hearts can do that. I've consulted mine; it will take its chances with the rosenkavalier."

"Oh, Suzanne, bless you! You've made a very sensible decision." She hugged her eldest.

"Sensible! But have you, Mother? The summer is almost over and George may not come again."

Mrs. Margot paced. "Six years, six years," she accused her image in the mirror. "The lines won't stay this fine forever."

"And judging from his hairline neither will George's hair."

"What a horrid thing to say," responded Mrs. Margot without conviction.

Betty rushed into the kitchen. "Mama, what's keeping the coffee? You haven't heard about George's vice-president in charge of exploration back from Alaska and tall, attractive, and divorced!"

"No, dear, I've been hearing about George's hairline."

"George's what? Really, Mama, this day has been too much for you."

"No, dearest, not at all. His hairline has quite revived me. George has shown the sense to have a high forehead."

Betty gave her mother a look, sidelong and strange. *I'll* make the coffee. You'd better save the men from the boredom of Nancy's saga. She goes on and on about Charles."

And Eleanor Margot, with a not unbecoming giggle of delight, linked arms with Suzanne and almost danced into the living room.

THE END

About the Author

SONDRA LUGER taught English in a New York City high school.

She enjoys art, opera, jazz, classical music (especially Mozart, Haydn and Handel) and literature (Jane Austen is a favorite).

She believes in happy endings. "If you don't believe in them you'll never have them; if you believe, you have a chance. Whatever I do I aim for a challenging trip, a happy ending and a positive effect on the lives of others." She dabbles at tennis and golf. "Winning is not the point."

Her home is in Westchester, New York.

www.ingramcontent.com/pod-product-compliance
Lightning Source LLC
Chambersburg PA
CBHW070949190726
48292CB00004B/1391